LIGHTHOUSE DREAMS

Jen, Sis,

You are the most beautiful person I know. I hope you enjoy the book. It's finally out.

Follow Your Dreams.

Maria

LIGHTHOUSE DREAMS

Marica Vance

TATE PUBLISHING
AND ENTERPRISES, LLC

Lighthouse Dreams
Copyright © 2014 by Marica Vance. All rights reserved.

No part of this publication may be reproduced, stored in a retrieval system or transmitted in any way by any means, electronic, mechanical, photocopy, recording or otherwise without the prior permission of the author except as provided by USA copyright law.

This novel is a work of fiction. Names, descriptions, entities, and incidents included in the story are products of the author's imagination. Any resemblance to actual persons, events, and entities is entirely coincidental.

The opinions expressed by the author are not necessarily those of Tate Publishing, LLC.

Published by Tate Publishing & Enterprises, LLC
127 E. Trade Center Terrace | Mustang, Oklahoma 73064 USA
1.888.361.9473 | www.tatepublishing.com

Tate Publishing is committed to excellence in the publishing industry. The company reflects the philosophy established by the founders, based on Psalm 68:11,
"The Lord gave the word and great was the company of those who published it."

Book design copyright © 2014 by Tate Publishing, LLC. All rights reserved.
Cover design by Nikolai Purpura
Interior design by Jimmy Sevilleno

Published in the United States of America
ISBN: 978-1-62994-363-3
Fiction / General
14.03.20

Acknowledgments

I WOULD LIKE TO thank my family for putting up with me while I try my hand at this new adventure. I would especially like to thank my spouse for proofreading for me, my daughter Katie for helping me learn to navigate the computer, and my daughter Shalee, for being my sounding board and letting me running ideas by her and the input that they both gave when I ran my ideas by them and asked for their opinions. Finally I'd like to thank Tate Publishing for taking a chance on me and giving me this opportunity to pursue my dream. My biggest blessing on this adventure came from my editor, helping me and advising me on what I need to do.

Table of Contents

Prologue	9
Chapter One	13
Chapter Two	21
Chapter Three	26
Chapter Four	30
Chapter Five	34
Chapter Six	41
Chapter Seven	43
Chapter Eight	50
Chapter Nine	59
Chapter Ten	64
Chapter Eleven	69
Chapter Twelve	77
Chapter Thirteen	84
Chapter Fourteen	91
Chapter Fifteen	103
Chapter Sixteen	113
Chapter Seventeen	118
Chapter Eighteen	129
Chapter Nineteen	139

CHAPTER TWENTY	147
CHAPTER TWENTY-ONE	163
CHAPTER TWENTY-TWO	167
CHAPTER TWENTY-THREE	174
CHAPTER TWENTY-FOUR	179
CHAPTER TWENTY-FIVE	186
CHAPTER TWENTY-SIX	191
CHAPTER TWENTY-SEVEN	196
CHAPTER TWENTY-EIGHT	204
EPILOGUE	211

Prologue

ON A HILL along the East coast of Florida stood an old lighthouse that was very special to a thirteen year old girl named Susan. She lived in a small house not far from the lighthouse, yet a little too far for her to walk alone. Susan's best friend Andy had lived at the lighthouse until about two years ago. Oh! How she missed him. She would sneak off and go to the lighthouse every chance she got. There was a lot of stuff left in the lighthouse and she often wondered if it was from her friend's family. Susan loved to climb to the top where she would sit and dream while looking out over the ocean. She could sit there for hours at a time watching the ships pass. On one such visit she found herself dozing and the hour grew late as she awoke. Susan knew that she was going to have to sneak in when she got home and she just hoped her parents didn't catch her because she knew that they would be angry with her for stayingout so late.

Andy was a 14 year old boy named after his farther Anderson. He and his parents had lived in the lighthouse when he was a child, and his best memories from growing up were from that old lighthouse. Andy's dad was a very successful businessman when another small company asked him to help them get started. Unfortunately, this new opportunity meant that their family would have to move very far away. Andy didn't want to leave his friends especially his best friend Susan. The only part of the big move that even sounded fun was that they got to take a boat trip to get there. This job would require them to move across the ocean. Andy looked forward to the trip on the big ship as he had never been on a boat, much less a ship. As the years passed, Andy often recalled his excitement and how he couldn't wait to travel on the big ship to his new home. When the family made the trip, they left most of their belongings behind as they would only be gone for a year or two at the most. They boxed up most of their possessions and draped sheets over the furniture. When they got to the ship, it was huge. Andy was so excited; he didn't even get sea sick, but his Grandma did. The trip on the ship seemed to take forever. The excitement had worn off and he was tired of being stuck on the ship. Even worse was poor grandma as she had been sea sick the whole time. When there were only 2 more days in their journey a big storm came up and everyone was scared. Even the captain looked frightened, but he said it was nothing to worry about. The crew got out the life jackets and made everyone put them on. As the big ship took on water we were directed to get into the small boats that hung from the side of the ship. Somehow in the chaos Andy and his grandma were separated from his parents. His mom and dad were put into a different boat but they said it would be okay because they were right behind them. That was the last time Andy had seen his parents. Another ship had spotted them and was coming to help, but several people ended up missing. The crew searched and searched for the missing boats, but two of them and their passengers were never found. Among the missing were Andy's parents. His grandma being the kind of lady that she was had promised she would take care of him. She sent him to all of the best school and bought him everything that he could ever need. She was raising him into a fine young man.

CHAPTER ONE

Five years later.

SUSAN HAS JUST graduated high school and is a beautiful young woman. At 5foot 7inches she has curves in all of the right places, wavy brown hair is sun-kissed with natural highlights and eyes the color of melted chocolate that a man could find himself drowning in. As summer was just beginning her flawless skin was just developing a coppery glow. She didn't recognize how beautiful she truly was but she had started noticing that men would look her way as she passed by.

Despite the years Susan would still walk to the lighthouse regularly, often wondering if Andy would ever return. Her parents had told her about the ship going down and him losing his parents, but she knew that he and his grandma had been rescued. She had grieved for his loss when she heard and she often thought of the times that she had spent with him and his parents at the lighthouse before his move. She would still climb the lighthouse steps from time to time to watch the ships pass, once she had even seen a pod of dolphins playing in the waves.

Andy had promised he would return someday, but they were so young then, and after the accident Susan had her doubts. While she had pretty much given up hope of ever seeing her childhood friend again, she wondered if he ever thought of her or missed the lighthouse. While she didn't get to visit the lighthouse as much as she would like, due to school and life, Susan still tried to come by at least once a week. This place was and always would be her special place, she knew that she could always come here to dream, or even just think.

On this visit Susan noticed there were some changes to the lighthouse and she wondered what was going on. Items were missing and it looked like it was being cleaned up. She had never noticed anyone while she was here. No one had been around for years as far as she knew. No one had any idea that she would come and go as she pleased. While Susan knew it may be trespassing for her to climb those steps, as far as she was concerned it was her lighthouse. While hoping and praying all these years that Andy would return one day, she had somehow claimed this place as her own.

Whoever had been there was going through things and cleaning out, she hoped they didn't plan on tearing her lighthouse down. Just the idea of losing the lighthouse devastated her. She had found all kinds of treasures, as she thought of them, as well as pictures of Andy and his family. She found herself, as she so often did, wondering what had happened to him.

Susan found herself pulled from her reflection by a sound from below. Suddenly all of her mother's warnings came back to her. She sat very still listening until she heard it again. "Oh no!" she wondered what to do when a light came on in the house down below.

Someone was in there but she had been so caught up in her thoughts and reflections that she hadn't heard them come in. She peered over the rail from her perch and sure enough there was a car in the driveway. How in the world had she not heard it pull in? Now she was scared, how was she going to get down and out the door without being seen? Slowly Susan made her way down the stairs, planning her escape. Halfway down, she froze; there was a man but his back was to her. Slowly she lowered herself to the step watching what he was doing. She sat waiting for him to turn around so she could see what he looked like. The stairwell was dark around her as he only had a small lamp lit. He was looking through the photos and objects around him when he finally turned enough that she could see his profile. Oh my, he was handsome and she felt a funny flutter in her stomach. He looked young, not much older than she was. There was something familiar about him, maybe she had seen him before?

Although Susan felt sure she would remember him if she had ever seen him. He was tall maybe around six foot. He had broad shoulders and his hair was dark brown, nearly black. From where she sat, his eyes looked dark, but she couldn't really tell, and his skin had the pale appearance of one who spends more time inside than in the sun. She felt a compulsion to get closer, but she was afraid to move. Oh, but he did look good to her.

Susan battled an internal war in those moments, *What to do? Maybe I can get just a little closer? What if he catches me, what would he do? It is dark here on the steps* and he is all the way over there looking through the stuff that was left here. Who is he? she thought and why is he boxing everything up?

She moved down to the bottom step as he started moving towards her. *Wait, he couldn't have heard me! I was quiet,* she thought. Little did she know that he had known she was there.

Andy could smell Susan and she smelled so good to him. She smelled like spring with a hint of the sea. He had caught a whiff of her scent and it had given her away. He had been looking at an old picture of his mom and dad when he thought he heard someone. He just didn't know that it was a female until he caught her scent. He started moving things around while he made his way slowly towards the stairs. He was hoping to make it to the stairs before he scared her off as he had a few questions for her.

Andy needed to know who this mystery woman was. How had she gotten in and why was she here?

Just as he got close enough to grab her, she bolted through the door. He tried to catch hold of her arm but he fell over some boxes and missed. Cursing he got up and ran after her. By the time he got out of the house she was running up the beach. *Man she's fast,* he thought. She glanced over her shoulder and he got his first real look at her. *Wow! She is beautiful,* he thought. She was wearing a light green bikini top and matching short shorts. Her long brown hair hung in a braid down her back that flew out behind her as she ran on some of the longest legs he had ever seen.

As Susan turned back to look for him, she fell. He hoped that she was okay but as he got closer he noticed that she wasn't getting up and he picked up his pace. He knelt down beside her and she started to move. Andy reassured her, "Lay still, I won't hurt you, I just want to make sure that you are okay." She grew very still and quiet as she looked into the eyes of the most handsome man she had ever seen.

He wasn't like any of the guys that she knew, not that she dated a lot. She had dated a few guys but that was in high school. He had dark blue eyes the color or the deepest part of the ocean, and his face was covered with a day's growth of stubble the same dark shade as his hair. His well-defined muscular arms and chest led her to believe that he works out.

Andy bent down to check her ankle and Susan was caught off guard by the tingle that shot up her leg and the pain in her ankle. She yelled, "Stop touching me!" Andy explained, "I'm only trying to see if you broke it." As he was turning her ankle his gaze drifted up her leg and she said, "My ankle is down there, now let me up." He laughed and said, "No, I think not." Andy admired her spirit.

"Excuse me, who are you and why were you in my house?"

"You're House?" She asked.

"Yes I used to live there when I was younger. We moved away; but now that I'm grown, I've moved back."

"So you're the young boy in all those pictures?"

"I see you've been snooping," he said.

She blushed and said "well, no one has lived there for years and I love going to the top just to sit and watch the ocean."

Andy laughed and confided, "Yes I always liked doing that too. Now you never did tell me your name?"

"It's Susan, why?"

"Well I may need to report a robbery."

"That's not fair! I didn't take anything! I just like going up to the top. I always have, ever since I was younger. How old were you when you moved away?" She asked.

Andy laughed saying, "Easy there, Susan; I was only kidding. You answered my questions, now I will answer yours."

They sat there on the beach and became reacquainted, realizing that they were the long lost friends each had longed for. Andy told Susan what had happen and how his grandma had raised him and about why he couldn't come back. Susan was so happy to see Andy again and she couldn't believe how handsome he had become.

The longer they sat there, the more Andy wanted to kiss her. *Lord she was beautiful, he* thought.

"I should have come back a long time ago" he said.

She blushed a little and let out a nervous giggle.

Finally, before he did something to scare her off, he said, "Let me help you up."

She gave him her hand and when he took it, a spark run up both of their arms.

He asked, "Susan would you like to come up for a drink, and maybe I could drive you home?"

"No, I better not, I should be getting home."

Susan started walking down the beach with a slight limp he hoped she didn't have to go far. He couldn't remember how far it was to her house and he would have loved to take her home so he could see where she lived.

Andy called towards her retreating back, "May I call on you?"

"You better not just yet, but I'll come back tomorrow."

Andy stood there and watched her go knowing he had to see her again.

Susan limped off down the beach wading out into the water a little as she went. She walked for a long time thinking of Andy and how good he looked now. She didn't think to ask him how old he was now and she couldn't remember how much of an age difference there was between them. He looked like he was in his early twenties but she wasn't good at judging ages.

Susan walked longer than she had planned, but she didn't want him to follow her. Although she knew him when they were younger, a lot had changed and she didn't know what her parents would say. She didn't think they would like her being at the lighthouse alone with him when they didn't know him very well as an adult.

Susan's parents thought she had stopped going to the lighthouse years ago, she just never told them she still went there. She knew they were right to worry and she shouldn't go there anymore, but she loved the old lighthouse. She didn't know what she would do now that Andy was back. She knew it was his home, but he had been away from it so many years she hoped he didn't plan to sell it, or worse, have it torn down. Yes, it was old and in need of repairs which would require a lot of money, but the idea of losing her lighthouse made her heart heavy.

Andy seemed like a nice enough guy and he sure was handsome, but she didn't know how well off he was in the financial area. It would take a long time to get all of the necessary repairs done right. She wished that she could help as she had always dreamed of fixing the place up. Oh! How she wanted to be the one to live there. She could remember thinking a few years ago of how she would fix it up and decorate each room. It would be so pretty and the light at the top would be the first thing that she would replace. It would be lit with a very bright light that would shine for miles so all the ships could see. She could sit up there all night if she wanted to and she would have a small table and chairs there to sit and share the view with someone special.

Susan rounded a corner on the beach and she could see home. She went in through the back door into the kitchen and grabbed a snack on her way to her bedroom.

Chapter Two

ANDY STARTED BACK to the house as he watched her walk away, down the beach. He still had so many unanswered questions. He was kicking himself for not asking her last name, it had been so many years that he had forgotten what it was. He didn't think she was married but he hadn't asked that either, or even where she lived now.

Andy found himself reveling at her beauty and the connection between them. He couldn't help but to think of how slim her legs were as he had checked her ankle. As soon as he touched her he had felt a fire in his veins, it was like nothing he had ever experienced before. Even now, he felt the warmth pulsing through him. He chuckled at the memory of her anger when she caught his gaze wandering up her legs. He bet she was a firecracker when she really got mad. While he wasn't trying to upset her, he couldn't help admiring her gorgeous legs. Just thinking about Susan filled him with the fire of desire. It had been too long since he had been with a woman.

He glanced back for one last look as she walked away, she was pretty far off and he found himself wondering how far she lived. While he could stand here watching her retreating back until she was out of sight, right now he had to get back to the lighthouse to get some more work done. He had just gotten back into town yesterday and had come straight here. He hadn't realized how much of a mess his former home would be.

He had not thought about the upkeep or the ramifications of letting it go for so long. It would take him ages to get this place back in order. He had loved this place as a boy and he had every intention of returning it to its former glory. He knew that living here would help him feel closer to his mom and dad. While Andy loved his grandma, she was a grand lady and had done a great job raising him, he missed his parents something awful and had never gotten over their deaths. He always wanted to come back here but grandma didn't want to.

Grandma had gotten so seasick on the initial trip, and then with losing his parents on that voyage, Andy couldn't blame her. She had tried her best to make him stay but she knew he was ready to be on his own and that he had grown into a fine young man. Upon his twenty-first birthday Grandma had transferred his trust fund from his parents into his name and added some to it . She had told him she knew he would do the right thing with the money or she would make the trip over there just to clobber him. He knew she meant it to. She was a good woman but when she said something like that you knew she meant business. He couldn't complain much though, she had always made sure he had food to eat, clothes to wear, and a clean place to live.

Andy went back into the lighthouse but he couldn't decide where to begin. He sat down and started sorting through things in the living room. He made a pile of items to get rid of and another pile of things to keep. Later, he would sort those items and put them away where they belonged. He worked late into the night not even realizing he had missed supper. There wasn't much in the house to eat since he hadn't stopped in town on his way in; but he had cheese, crackers, and a coke from the station where he last stopped for gas. He made do with that, planning a trip into town for groceries and cleaning supplies first thing tomorrow morning.

Andy decided to sleep on the old couch since he still needed to buy new sheets and towels. Despite his exhaustion, sleep didn't come easy as he lay there thinking about Susan. Eventually sleep overcame him only to dream of her.

In the morning, Andy headed straight to the diner to eat a real breakfast. As it turned out, the lady who owned the diner had known his parents. His quick stop at the diner turned into a couple hours of reminiscing. After his long breakfast he headed to the department store to pick up towels, sheets, blankets, and a few other essential so he could start really cleaning. From the department store he was off to the hardware store, and finally a quick stop to pick up groceries, he wanted more than cheese and crackers for supper tonight.

Andy would have to sleep on that old couch again since he hadn't bought a new bed yet. He wished he'd thought to stop at the furniture store to buy a bed yesterday while he was in town; that old couch wasn't comfortable.

After waking with an awful crick in his neck from that old couch, the next morning found Andy heading back into town to purchase a new bedroom suit and a few other essentials.

He couldn't wait for them to deliver and set his new bed up. He would finally get a good night's rest. Andy was impatiently awaiting the delivery when he heard a noise and saw the truck heading up the driveway. Once the bedroom was set up, Andy made his new bed and looked forward to a good night's sleep. As he looked around his bedroom his thoughts once again turned to Susan as he wondered what she was doing today? He hoped that she would stop by so he could invite her to have supper with him tonight.

Andy asked the delivery crew to take his parents' old bed away; for some reason he just couldn't sleep in it. It just didn't seem right, especially if he ever had a woman stay over. He also had them take away that horrible couch, he would definitely be buying a more comfortable one very soon.

Upon his return to the lighthouse, his thoughts immediately turned to Susan, it was late and he figured that he had probably already missed her today. Andy hoped not as he unloaded his truck and started his supper while putting the groceries away. He could put the rest away later. After his supper finished cooking, he decided to take it to the top of the lighthouse so he could look out over the ocean as he ate. Secretly he hoped Susan would be there. On his way up the steps he noticed that there were a few that needed replaced and he was surprised Susan hadn't got hurt going up and down them. He decided to fix them first thing in the morning. He didn't want Susan or anyone else to fall and hurt themselves. As he sat there eating he noticed a blanket over in the corner of the balcony, it must be Susan's, he thought. She said she loved it up here she must have left it here for when she got cold.

Andy could see why she loved being up here, you could see for miles in every direction. He looked towards the direction she went yesterday but he couldn't see any houses. Way off in the distance, he saw a few people on the beach and wondered if she was one of them. He stared out over the ocean thinking of his parents when out the corner of his eye he caught sight of something in the distance. As he focused on the movement he saw a pod of dolphins swimming and playing in the surf, it looked like they were having fun. In that moment that he knew he had done the right thing coming back.

He decided he was going to replace the lighthouse bulb right away, he wanted the ships to be able to see it if ever there was a need. The weather didn't often get bad here, but when it did, the ships would see it. He also wanted to pick up a couple of blankets, a small heater and maybe a small table for out here. After finishing his meal and relaxing for a while, Andy decided it was time to go back down stairs to clean up his mess.

Chapter Three

Susan hadn't seen Andy since the day he had caught her in the lighthouse. It had only been two days and she was trying to stay busy, but she couldn't help thinking about him. She had been helping her mom prepare for and host a birthday party for her little brother. Teddy had turned ten years old. Whew who knew watching all those little boys would be so exhausting? She was so glad it was over. They had spent all day today cleaning up from the party. The family had gotten up early so they could get the cleanup done before it got too hot. As they were finishing up, they saw a furniture truck headed down the road. They were Almost done when they saw a furniture truck go down the road. Susan's mom questioned where it could be headed but Susan didn't say anything because if she did her mom would know she was still going to the lighthouse. Susan's mom was a real sweetheart, easy to get along with and she loved her family above all else. She was very protective of them but only wanted the best for Susan and the rest of her family. She knew that Susan would often take long walks down the beach And she even knew that she was going to the lighthouse on these walks. While she didn't like it, at least no harm had come to her because the place was deserted.

Around two o'clock that afternoon they had finished and Susan asked her mom if she would mind if she went for a walk? Her mom smiled, "Don't be gone too long." Susan promised not to be too late and off she went. Susan could hardly wait; she wanted to see if he was moving out or what was going on. She ran half way then slowed down to walk the rest of the way just in case he happened to see her. As she got close enough to see, she saw stuff being loaded on to a truck. Susan didn't know whether to be mad or not. She didn't want Andy to move away. Susan didn't know how to feel. She didn't want Andy to move away! What if he tore it down or had decided to sell it? She didn't have the money to buy it herself and at her young age, she didn't have her credit established yet. She couldn't ask her parents to buy it they didn't have enough money. Oh! They had enough money that they were comfortable and she would never ask them to buy it for her. They would just laugh.

As she got to the truck she peeped inside the back and saw the couch, bed, and a lot of other stuff. She got so mad she ran inside and started yelling at Andy. Andy was in the middle of rearranging his table and chairs in place when she came through the door yelling. He thought something was wrong with her the way she was carrying on. She was talking so fast and and flailing her arms so much that he couldn't keep up, much less understand her. He slowly approached her, wrapping both his arms around her thinking that might calm her down. Oh man! Was he wrong she only got more carried away.

She yelled "Let me go!" Andy said "NO, not until you calm down and tell me what is wrong. Are you hurt? Is something wrong?" She stomped his toe, he yelled "Ouch! You little she-devil," as he picked her up and sat down in one of the kitchen chairs with her on his lap. She huffed and wiggled when suddenly she realized she was in his lap and that he was getting hard. She stopped wiggling at once and started catching her breath. Susan replied "You're moving again! You can't move!"

Andy laughed and said "I'm flattered you like me and don't want me to move."

"It's not that you…you..." she said stuttering

"Careful now, hon, you don't want to call me a bad name when you just admitted you like me and don't want me to leave."

"I did not" Susan said.

"Come on now not even a little," he said. "Now that I have your attention look around do you see anything different?"

She had stopped struggling and looked around, forgetting she was sitting in his lap. For the first time she saw where he had moved the old stuff out and was cleaning the floors and walls. Inquisitively she asked, "What are you doing?"

Andy had watched her as she looked around he loved the look of confusion on her face. He told her, "I'm getting rid of all the old stuff that isn't worth much, cleaning up and getting the place ready for some new furniture. The first thing I have to get is a new couch, that old one is rough! I slept on that thing for the last two nights and have a terrible crick in my neck."

Susan laughed with relief at his explanation. Andy reassured her, "See, I'm not leaving."

"Good," she said, and suddenly she realized she was still sitting on his lap. "Oh you can let me go now." "Are you sure?" Andy said, "I kind of like holding you, you're so soft and smell so sweet," as he nuzzled her neck.

She squirmed and giggled "Stop that, it tickles." But as she looked up into his eyes a warmth spread over her like she had never experienced. Suddenly she was overwhelmed with a desire to kiss him and he must have felt it too because every so slowly he leaned down and lightly brushed her lips with his so as not to scare her. Susan had never been kissed before and these sensations were all new to her. She liked the feeling of his lips on hers and as she parted her lips to speak he slipped his tongue into her mouth. She didn't know what to think at first, all these new strange feelings had started in her stomach. With her heart racing, she jumped from his lap and took off.

Chapter Four

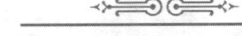

ANDY CALLED TO her, "Susan wait!," but it was too late. Susan was already half way down the beach. Man! He thought, I shouldn't have kissed her yet. She was like a scared kitten. He had to admit, he sure liked the taste of her on his lips. She had been so soft sitting in his lap, he bet she didn't weigh 100 pounds. While she certainly wasn't heavy, she had curves in all the right places. What an amazing set of breasts, she certainly had more than a handful!

"Oh well, guess I better get back to it or I won't get done." He had more work to do before he could go into town and pick out the rest of the furniture he needed. He also knew that he needed to get curtains, but he didn't have any idea how to coordinate them and was hoping to get Susan's input on that. If he hadn't scared her away he could be doing that now. Hopefully she would come back soon so he could ask for her help, if not he would figure it out on his own.

As Susan ran home she thought of Andy and his kiss, she could still feel his lips on hers. He was a very good kisser she would always remember it, especially since it was her first kiss. She really liked Andy and would love to get to know him better but his kiss had caught her off guard today. Crossing the backyard she saw her mom at the kitchen window so she went in the back door.

"Hi Mom," Susan said, "What's for supper?"

Her mom replied, "Chicken and dumplings, green beans, corn, and corn bread."

"Yum! That sounds good."

"Did you see where that big truck went earlier?" Her mom said.

Susan said, "Yes mom, it went to that old lighthouse someone must be moving in or clearing it out."

"Goodness," her mom said "No one has been there in years, not since that family moved away. You remember they had that young boy? You and he were best friends back then. Maybe you and I should take a walk up there later, and see what's going on."

Susan paled at the thought but replied, "Sure mom, whatever you want." Later that evening, after supper she helped her mom clean up and do the dishes. When they had everything done Susan headed up to her room and hoped her mother would forget about going to the lighthouse. She would have Teddy take his bath and get ready for bed. While she was busy with Teddy, her mom and dad could sit and relax in the living room. This was their normal nightly routine, they would talk of the things that had happened that day sometimes they would even take walks on the beach. Her mom loved the sound of the ocean and she guessed that's where she got it from.

As she started up the stairs, her mom stopped her, "Susan how about you and I take that walk now?

Your dad has other things on his mind." Turning to him she asked, "Derek is that all right with you?"

Derek absently replied "Yes dear, that will be fine."

Her mom, Patty, said, "Good, you make sure Teddy gets his bath while we are gone."

Derek sighed, "He will, now stop worrying."

So out the door they went and down to the beach. As they neared the lighthouse her mom remarked, "Look, there are some lights on in there. I bet someone is moving in."

Susan distractedly replied, "Yes, I think so too."

"So you have been walking up to the Lighthouse! Well?"

"Well what?" Susan asked.

"Did you get close enough to see anything??"

Susan hesitated, "I saw a young man but."

Her mom prompted, "Go ahead, I know you've been walking up there all along."

"You did?" Susan asked. "His name is Andy, I met him mom, it's the boy from the family that moved away, the one that I was friends with. He has finally decided to move back."

Patty questioned, "Well, what's he look like? How old is he now?"

Susan laughed, "Mom I'm not sure how old he is, I can't remember our age difference from before. He is tall and very handsome. His hair is the color of sand."

Her mom said "Um, huh, well now I know why you've been walking so much lately" and they both laughed. As they made their way back home her mom stated, "That settles it then, we will bake a cake in the morning and you can walk down here and bring it to him and welcome him back to the neighborhood. If he is staying he might just need help cleaning up and I just might go with you and check things out."

They laughed, and discussed what kind of cake to make. Susan slept great that night as she dreamt of Andy and their kiss. Even in her dreams she could feel his lips on hers.

She woke early the next morning and once again wondered what kind of cake to make. She thought maybe a carrot cake since it was her favorite, it might be his too? Maybe she would help him today with his cleaning if he asked her too. She would love to help him fix that place up it would be great to help bring it back to its' former glory, meanwhile she could pretend she was going to be living there too.

Chapter Five

ANDY GOT UP early this morning since he didn't sleep very well last night. All he could do was think unlike Susan of Susan, how soft she was and that kiss...he knew by her actions she was inexperienced but never had a kiss jolted him like that. He decided before dark today he would walk down the beach and try to find her maybe she would be walking his way or in her back yard and he would know where she lived then. Then he could introduce himself to her parents and see if he could call on her. Right now though, he needed to get a shower and some breakfast. After breakfast Andy decided to check the light up top and see what size he needed to pick up while he was in town. He had decided to start at the top and work his way down on restoring the lighthouse. He was going to paint, and then buy new furniture, lamps, decorations and such. By the time he started buying the decorative elements he knew he was going to need a woman's touch. He hoped Susan would be willing to help him. He headed to the hardware store up the road to get a light bulb for the lighthouse. Maybe he could at least get that replaced and the stairs repaired and painted today.

As he returned home from his shopping he saw two people on his porch. Wondering who it was he quickly pulled into his driveway and he could see one of his visitors was Susan the other an older woman, maybe be her mom? Andy parked his car and ran up the steps to the front porch. "Hello Ladies, how are you today Susan and who is this lovely lady with you?"

Hello Andy," Susan said, "This is my mom Patty."

Patty reached out to shake his hand and responded "Nice to see you again. My, you have grown up since the last time I saw you."

"Andy we brought you a carrot cake" Susan said,

"Yum that sounds good. I love carrot cake."

Patty had been watching the whole exchange. Yes, she thought Susan had been here and talked with him before today. She noticed the way Andy couldn't take his eyes off of Susan and how Susan wouldn't meet his gaze. Yes, Patty thought, he looks smitten with her and I can tell Susan was smitten with him.

Andy was thrilled to see Susan and he invited them in. Andy thanked them for the cake and invited them to have a piece and a cup of coffee. As they sat at the table eating Andy told them about all of the things he had been working on in the house. He told them what had happened when they moved away, about his grandma raising him, and how he got his trust fund at 21. He said he had always wanted to come back and the time was finally right. He explained about his business and how he could do it here or anywhere really with minimal travel.

After Andy had finished filling Susan and Patty in on his life, Patty told him what she remembered about his parents. She told him how horrible they felt when they heard about the tragedy.

She went on to explain that they didn't know if he had survived or not. "You know what Andy your mom and I were good friends. We used to walk together on the beach regularly. We spent a lot of time together until we had our children, then it seemed we were too busy taking care of y'all to really get together. After you came along, we would talk on the phone a lot. That's how we stayed in touch, we'd talk about our children and what was happening in town."

Andy said, "Maybe someday you can tell me more about her,"

Patty responded "Of course! I would love too."

Andy asked, "Susan how old are you?"

"I just turned 18."

"I see."

"How old are you," Susan inquired?

"I'm twenty-one. Patty, may I call on your daughter?"

"I'm sure you two have been getting to know each other already, but why don't you come over tomorrow night for supper? I'm sure it's been a long time since you've had a home-cooked meal."

"Yes ma'am it has and thank you I would love too."

"Good then Susan's father can get reacquainted with you and see how well you have turned out, then you can ask him about calling on Susan." She laughed saying "I'm sure it won't be a problem but it will also be up to Susan."

"Umm, yes ma'am" he replied, looking over at Susan. She looked thrilled. "Patty, would you mind if Susan helped me out with picking paint and furniture, carpets, curtains, that kind of stuff. I want this place to look like a warm, welcoming home. I have no idea where to start and I would really like a woman's perspective.

"That would be fine if Susan wants to, but you'll have to ask her."

He turned to Susan asking, "What about it? Are you game?"

"Sure I would love too, it will be fun to restore this place."

Susan couldn't believe everything that was happening. She had just planned to bring him a cake, now he was coming for supper and she was going to help him shop for and decorate the lighthouse. She was giddy about him coming to supper and that he was going to ask her dad if he could call on her.

I'm 18, I don't need his permission but it was nice that he was going to ask anyway. Susan was pulled back from her thoughts by their talking and laughing. As she glanced over at them, Andy caught her gaze, she smiled and blushed. Her mom caught the exchange and thought, there is a romance blooming here and she loved the idea of Susan and Andy together. Patty's thoughts turned to Andy's mom and she wished that she could be here to see this budding romance. Patty excused herself and was preparing to leave when Andy asked if Susan could stay awhile so he could show her what all he had planned for the lighthouse. Patty agreed with the plan and headed home. Glancing back, Patty called out "Supper tomorrow will be at seven o'clock, don't be late!" They both yelled, "OK!" as she walked off towards the beach.

As Patty made her way down the beach, they turned and head back inside the lighthouse. Susan asked, "So, what did you want to show me?"

Andy laughingly replied, "You better watch out, that's a loaded question." Susan laughed and they got to work in the living room. Susan made a list of their color selections and talked about what sort of stuff he wanted to put in the rooms. As they made their way through the house she continued to add to her list until the only rooms left were the bedrooms. By the time they had finished making all their choices and notes it was late afternoon. Andy decided that they should wait until tomorrow to go into town and he asked Susan if she would like to go with him to help pick things out. She responded, "Sure, I would love too."

Since they were done for today, they headed up to the top and he told her he had ordered a new bulb for the light so he could light it up again. Susan was excited to hear he would be restoring the light. As they reached the top she noticed he now had a cooler there as he opened it and took out a coke for them to share while they sat there looking out over the ocean talking. Susan asked him how he felt about going through some of the old photos and picking some to hang up. She told him, "Maybe a family photo would help you feel closer to your parents." He replied, That's a great idea, just being back here is doing just that."

They headed back down into the house to go through his photos. Susan found one of him as a little boy and they both laughed. He picked out several photos of him growing up, including one of him and his dad fishing. They decided they would take them into town with them tomorrow and have a collage made up.

Finished with the pictures, Andy said, "Let's go upstairs to the bedrooms and decide what colors to paint them, then we should get going to your house. I don't want to keep you here too late." Susan laughed. After they decided on the colors of the spare bedrooms they headed into his bedroom. "What's your favorite color?", Susan asked. She couldn't believe how big his bedroom was. "You have a huge bed." He laughingly replied, "Yeah after sleeping on that couch I wanted a big bed." The room was huge with lots of windows facing toward the ocean, it also had a big walk-in closet. Off to the side was a master bathroom and another door.

Susan questioned, "What's this door to?"

"I hope someday it will be a nursery."

"OH! Let's do it in pastels then."

"OK, we can pick up everything we need tomorrow."

"I better head home so we can get an early start tomorrow."

Andy walked her home so he could see where she lived and would know where to come tomorrow. As they walked up to the house, Patty stuck her head out the back door and told Andy, "Thanks for walking her home." He replied, "You're welcome. Do you mind if Susan goes to town with me in the morning to help pick out some curtains, rugs, and furniture? According to Susan, I need more in a bedroom than just a bed." Patty laughed, "I agree with Susan on that. You can pick her up anytime." Andy stepped onto the back porch

with Susan and told her, "I will pick you up at seven, if that is ok?" Susan said, "That would be fine" as Andy leaned in and gave her a lite kiss whispering,
 "Goodnight."

Chapter Six

SUSAN WALKED IN the back door as her lips were tingling from their kiss. She wondered if he put something on his lips to cause this strange sensation. Shrugging it off; she walked into the kitchen where her mom was preparing some of the dishes for supper tomorrow night.

"Oh no," Susan said "I need to stay here in the morning to help You."

"Nonsense! I can cook for one extra person just fine, I always have when one of yours or Teddy's friends ended up staying all night at the last minute. At least I know he is coming ahead of time so I can prepare some of it tonight. Now, don't just stand there, start peeling potatoes."

Susan laughingly replied, "Okay", she knew her mom hated peeling potatoes so she didn't mind helping out. They worked together to get most of the cooking done that night. The women made deviled eggs, potato salad, baked beans, asparagus casserole, and chocolate pies. Finally after all of the sides were ready, they put the ham into the oven before they went to bed.

Surveying their work, Susan exclaimed, "Mom he is just one man, we really don't need a feast!"

Patty laughed saying, "Yes, but he could be the right one. Susan haven't you seen the way he looks at you?"

Susan didn't let her mother's words sink in before replying, "I better head off to bed it is going to be a long day tomorrow. He's picking me up at 7am"

"I see," said Patty, "then you'd better get off to bed, you've never have been one to get up that early."

Susan laughed saying, "Goodnight then.

Chapter Seven

Andy walked back home while thinking of Susan and the events of the day. She was such a pretty little thing and smart too. They seem to like a lot of the same things so far. He really loved the way she thought of the family photo idea and the way she laughed. He could listen to her laugh all day. He couldn't wait to meet her dad and ask his permission to call on her. He wants to get to know her a lot better so far he loved what he knew. Lost in his thoughts, it didn't take him very long to make the walk back to the lighthouse. Before long He was home, he headed upstairs to take a shower, then ate a snack and headed to bed.

The next morning Andy got up ate a quick breakfast and headed out to pick up Susan. He could hardly wait to see her again she had filled his dreams all night. Just thinking about her made him want to kiss her again her lips were so full and inviting. He could clearly recall how it felt when she sat on his lap and the light kiss they had shared. He wanted to hold her in his arms and give her a real kiss so badly. He pulled up to her house, just as Susan was coming out the front door. He couldn't take his eyes off her as she came down the front steps and got into the truck, "Good morning, Beautiful." She was thrilled that he thought she looked beautiful, as she had taken extra care when getting ready this morning. She wanted to look just right for him and wore a light blue dress since she now knew it was his favorite color. She had chosen white sandals, and a simple pearl necklace with matching earrings to go with the dress.

Susan replied, " Good morning, Andy. Where to first?"

"I thought the furniture store first what do you think?"

Susan agreed, that way they could decide how to arrange the rooms which would help them in picking out the paint, carpet, and curtains.

Andy chuckled, "if you say so. I'm glad you like this sort of thing."

Susan laughingly replied, "Don't you think your girlfriend would like to help you with this sort of thing?" While she didn't think he was married, he didn't wear a ring, she was certain that he must have already have a girlfriend.

Andy sighed, "I kind of thought she was helping me, unless you don't want to be my girlfriend?"

Susan felt her face grow hot as she blushed, "I would love to be your girlfriend if you're sure."

Andy quickly responded, "Hon, I have never wanted anyone as much as I want you."

They pulled into the parking lot of the furniture Store and Andy asked her to stay put while he got out and went around the truck to help her get out. The truck was a little high and he didn't want her to get hurt so he wanted to help her down. As she started to get out, she turned towards him and he caught a glimpse of her leg. She had great legs he would never get tired of looking at them. As they walked into the furniture store he told her to pick out whatever she liked as money was no object.

Susan asked, "Are you sure?" Her family lived well but they had to watch their money, she wasn't used to spending money this freely. As they walked around the store, they talked about his style and what items they should get. A sales lady who knew Susan, approached them, asking how she could help. They started with the living room

Next they picked out a beautiful bedroom suite for the extra bedroom. Finally they finished with his bedroom, since he already had a bed they found the one he had already purchased and selected the matching dresser. Susan also talked him into getting a lounge chair for in front of the double glass doors in his bedroom. It was big enough for two people to lie on comfortably and enjoy the view. Andy loved it, he had to admit he never would have thought of it. They also selected night stands for either side of the bed. Susan picked out some lamps that had a little blue in them so they would fit in with her plans for the bedroom.

Andy suggested, "As far as the nursery we can just paint and puts curtains up for now." When he saw a pretty rocker he asked, "Susan do you like this?"

She told him that she thought it was very pretty, so he got it too. He told Susan it fit her, he could just see her sitting in it rocking a baby. Susan was caught off guard by his statement. Her face lit up, she couldn't believe he was thinking of that already. Sure she liked him, but wow just wow. She knew she liked him, a lot, but she didn't know for sure how he felt. She really hoped things would work out for them, he was so gorgeous and those eyes. She could just melt every time she looked into his eyes.

After they finished up at the furniture store they headed to the paint store where they picked out all the paint colors and grabbed brushes, rollers, and a couple of ladders. From the paint store, they headed to the department store to finish up their shopping. Going into the store, Susan saw a lot of her friends that worked there. They all called out, "Hi" and she stopped to say "hello as well." Andy laughed and accused, "You just wanted to come see all your friends."

Susan laughed and said, "You bet I did! I wanted to show you off."

"Is that right? Well let's give them a real show then," he grabbed her before she knew what he was planning. He tilted her head back and slowly leaned down to kiss her. He intended it to be short and playful, but as soon as their lips connected and he tasted her he couldn't get enough of her. She was a perfect fit in his arms and he didn't want to let her go. She parted her lips a little and he pushed his tongue inside her sweet mouth. Her legs went weak, as their tongues danced, she wrapped her arms around his neck. He broke it off breathing heavy,

"We'd better stop before I can't." She was so weak. He had to steady her before letting go.

Susan laughed as she was overcome with joy. Once they were both recovered, they filled up two shopping carts with the items that he would need to make his house a home. They picked out sheets, blankets, pillows, lamps, towels, and anything else they could think of. Just as they were finishing up, Andy told her, "I only have paper plates, bowls, and cups." So they picked out plates, silverware, glasses, and serving dishes, as well as some pots and pans.

Andy made one more stop to pick up the light bulb he had ordered for the lighthouse. Susan was so excited about fixing the light, she couldn't wait till it was working again. They had made arrangements for all of the furniture to be delivered in two days so they would have time to get everything painted first. Andy suggested that they grab some lunch since all that shopping had made him hungry. Susan agreed and they stopped at a small diner to get burgers and cokes. Susan warned him not to eat too much because her mom had cooked a feast.

"I wish she hadn't gone to all that trouble," Andy sighed.

"She always does, especially when someone comes," Susan explained.

As they ate their quick lunch, Susan filled him in on the rest of her childhood after he had left.

She regaled him with stories about her life, growing up, about her brother Teddy, and her dad.

Finished with lunch, they headed back to the lighthouse.

Susan exclaimed, "Oh no we forgot something!"

He questioned, "What could we have possibly forgot?"

She laughed and said, "A washer and dryer."

While he couldn't argue with that, he asked, "Can it wait a couple days? That way we will have another excuse to go back into town if your dad won't let me date you."

She laughed and replied, "I suppose so. as long as you have enough clean clothes to last until then."

The man at the paint store had told them to get everything painted before the carpet was installed and the furniture would be delivered. So they decided to start painting first thing in the morning. With any luck they could get it all done in a couple days.

He knew that it would be easier to wait a few days, than having it delivered too soon when they would have to move it all around and cover it. This way they wouldn't get anything on it. They assured him that the delay would not be a problem.

As they pulled up to Susan's house, he told her, "I will drop you off and be back in time for supper. I need some time to clean up and get ready."

She said, "Okay I'll see you soon," and headed into the house.

After their busy day, Susan decided to take a quick nap so she would be refreshed for tonight. Lying in bed, she thought of the kiss that he planted on her and in front of her friends. What would they say?

Who cares? It was so good, she thought, she could kiss him all day long. He was such a good kisser. She had never been kissed like that and the memories filled her thoughtsas she drifted off to sleep to dream of Andy.

Susan awoke to a knock on her bedroom door.

"Mom says you better get up and get ready. It won't be long until that guy is here," called Teddy.

Susan laughed, "His name is Andy."

"Whatever, you better get up and get ready."

"Okay!" she yelled down to see if her mom needed any help?

"No, but you better get ready."

Susan jumped up and prepared to take a quick bath. Susan had no idea what to wear.

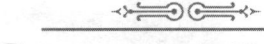

Chapter Eight

ANDY DROVE ON home thinking of the day he had just spent with Susan and how much he enjoyed her company. She showed great taste on everything they had picked out. As he drove up the drive he noticed all the work that he was having done on the outside was coming along really good. It really looked great

He knew they were nearly done and he couldn't wait to put in the new light bulb and light it up. After he and Susan finished setting up and decorating inside, he would ask for her help picking out some flowers and plants for around the outside. He wanted to make it look more like a home and he thought she would probably like picking out the flowers.

Once all of the repairs and updates were done, he looked forward to sitting on the top balcony, next to the light, eating supper, and watching for dolphins. He couldn't believe how similar they still were but she seemed like she was hiding something, or she was just awful shy, he couldn't decide. He went inside so he could get a few things done before he had to get ready to go to Susan's.

Andy drove over to Susan's house and started up to the door. Just as he started to knock a young boy opened the door, turning his head, he yelled, "He's here!" Patty came to the door and scolded Teddy for yelling before she introduced them. "Andy this is my son Teddy with the big mouth."

Andy laughed, and said, "Hi Teddy," as he shook his hand.

Patty said, "come on in, I'll show you to the den where Derek is."

As they entered the den, Derek stood up and Patty introduced them and they shook hands. Derek said, "Have a seat young man would you like a drink?" Derek was a nicely dressed man.

"Yes sir, a scotch would be fine." Derek fixed him a drink. Sitting down, they started talking about the weather. Then Derek asked him what line of work he was in. Andy was distracted, looking around wondering when Susan would be down, and he missed the question.

Upstairs, Susan was finishing up getting ready. She had chosen a pale green dress, with a Silver Star necklace. She wore her hair up tonight, as she thought it made her look at least a year older. Choosing a pair of silver sandals, she headed down stairs where she heard voices in the den. As she opened the door Andy looked her way, he stood up and walked over to her whispering, "Susan you look stunning," he leaned over to kiss her cheek. Her dad coughed to remind them that they weren't alone.

Derek said, "Susan, please join us." They all took a seat just as Patty walked in. Looking to Andy, Derek asks, "Well now that we are all here Andy, what is it you wanted to talk to me about?"

Andy cleared his throat, "Sir, I would like to call on your daughter and date her, if she agrees, that is."

When Derek hesitated to reply, Patty interceded, "Derek, stop torturing the young man."

Derek laughed and said "I see no problem with it, if Susan wants to go out with you, it is really up to her; but she must be home by midnight."

Andy said, "That won't be a problem, sir," and grinned over at Susan as she lowered her head, a blush lighting up her cheeks.

"By the way, the fact that your mother and Patty were such good friends is the only reason I said yes so fast, but I expect you to act as a gentleman while you are out with my daughter."

"Yes sir, I will!"

As the conversation turned to other topics, Patty announced, "Well now that is out of the way, supper is ready, if y'all are hungry?" They made their way into the dining room, her mom and dad set at the ends of the table, with Teddy on one side and Susan and Andy on the other. Andy liked her younger brother Teddy, they got along pretty well and he seemed to be a nice young lad.

After the meal, Andy thanked Patty for the wonderful meal as well as for the cake they had brought him the other day. The group retired to the den for after-dinner drinks and talked of his plans for the lighthouse. After a while, Andy, noticing that it was growing late, started to make his goodbyes, "I better be going," he didn't want to overstay his welcome. Andy asked Susan to walk him out.

Out on the porch, he said, "Your dad is really nice."

"Yes he is, but would you have thought so if he had told you we couldn't see each other."

Andy laughed, "I would have seen you anyways, if you would have let me."

"Oh, I would have!"

Pulling her into his arms, Andy asked, "So do you agree to date me and only me, until we see if we are meant for each other and we see where this leads?"

Susan looked into his eyes and watched the passion building there, "Yes, I do."

He pulled her into his arms for a kiss. As she wrapped her arms around his neck, the kiss deepened and he wrapped his arms more tightly around her groaning. She was so sweet, he was on fire for her. She melted in his arms wondering if he was feeling this fire building in him like she did. They kissed until they were both breathless and weak-kneed. Catching her breath Susan pleaded, "Don't stop," and pulled him back into her arms. As their kiss deepened, she moaned and he let out a low growl. He broke away, "Susan your killing me! I want you so bad. I fear if I don't stop now, I won't be able too. I want our first time to be special and perfect for you. I'd love to drag you to my truck right now and finish this, but that isn't what either of us really wants. I think you know, I have strong feeling for you, even if we've only gotten reacquainted over the last few days. There is a real connection here and I feel like we are meant to be, but I want us both to be sure when we take this step. I don't want you to have any regrets. You are, we are, much too important to me to throw it all away on one impulsive moment. We need to wait just a little longer, until it is right for both of us, because I don't want to lose you now that I finally have you back in my life!"

Still feeling unsettled and breathless from their kisses, she told him that she understood what he was saying, and agreed, even though she really didn't want to stop. She would have to think on all of this tonight while she was alone in her room. She didn't understand all these strange new feelings she was experiencing. She was tingling all over, hot one minute, then embarrassed the next. She knew that she wanted him more than she had ever wanted anyone in her life, but why? What was causing this pull inside of her, this wantonness that she had never experienced before? One thing was for sure, she didn't want Andy to think she was loose, and she didn't want to risk ruining their budding relationship by rushing things. She knew that if they waited, it would be even better when they came together, but this fire inside her was threatening to consume her.

One thing for sure she didn't want Andy to think she was a slut. Andy said, but we have to stop or your dad will be out here with his shotgun.

Andy seeing the confusion on Susan's face and knowing that he had to be the one to stop things before it was too late said, "Please, don't think that I am doing this because I don't want you, because I want you more than you so bad it physically hurts right now. We have to stop though, or your dad will be out here with his shotgun chasing me off permanently. Will you come over tomorrow and help me paint?"

"Do you even have to ask? Yes, I will be there! Until tomorrow, I will dream of you and our kisses."

"Darling, I hope you do because you have been in my dreams since the day I caught you in my lighthouse."

Susan blushed, "Well I guess I'll see you tomorrow then."

As Andy drove off Susan went back inside and was met by her father and mother, at the door. Her dad jokingly said, "I thought for a second that I was going to have to arrange a wedding, as long as it took y'all to say goodbye.

Susan felt her cheeks flaming up again, "Oh Dad! What did you think of him?"

"He seems like a nice young man. I think y'all make a good pair, but now honey, I don't want you two moving too fast on this. It takes time to get to know people and you need to be sure before you make any decisions on long term plans."

Susan knew what her parents said was true, but she couldn't help these feeling that were growing in her since Andy had come home. She reassured her parents that she would take her time and they had nothing to worry about. Wanting to change the subject, she asked her mom if she needed help cleaning up from dinner.

Patty and Susan set about cleaning up the kitchen, clearing off the table and covering the leftovers to put in the refrigerator. As her mom worked on putting away the leftovers, Susan cleared the table and started washing the dishes. Her mom hated doing dishes, so Susan tried to do them for her as often as possible especially when she had company over. As they worked, Patty asked, "You really like him don't you Susan?"

"Yes mom, I think he is great, and so HOT."

Her mom laughed, "You're right about that."

Susan looked at her mom incredulously.

"What? I may be getting old but I'm not blind child!" Sharing a laugh, Mom told Susan, "I can finish up here, go on up and get ready for bed."

"Okay Mom, thanks! Goodnight, I love you."

Susan got ready for bed and slipped beneath the covers as thoughts of Andy raced through her mind. She knew sleep would elude her tonight, as she lay there thinking of the kisses they had shared outside. Wow! He sure knew how to kiss! He could make her toes curl, his kiss was so powerful. She had never experienced anything like this before but she loved the feelings his kisses stirred up in her.

He made her feel like a grown woman not like an 18 year old child. She knew he had probably dated older girls since he was 21 but she refused to allow herself to think about the other women. After all he had chosen to move back here and came alone so they must not have meant much to him. Susan was glad he moved back and wasn't married or had brought anyone with him. This gave her hope as she thought of that she drifted off to sleep dreaming of his kisses.

As Andy drove home he couldn't help but smile. The night had gone well, her dad gave his approval for him to date Susan. He knew he didn't have to ask, but felt it was more respectful to both her and her parents to ask. He didn't want to put Susan in a position to have to sneak around and he wanted the approval of her parents for their relationship. That way, should they get serious, and it seemed they might if those few kisses he had stolen tonight were any indication.

Losing his train of thought he could not help the way he felt when she had grabbed him, saying don't stop, and kissed him again. That lady had some spirit and he couldn't wait to explore it further. She would be like a flower opening for the first time. He wanted to be the person she opened up for, she had set him on fire tonight, he could still feel the blood racing through his veins. Never had he wanted another woman as much as he wanted Susan. If he had ever dreamed of her being back here waiting for him, he wouldn't have waited so long to move back home. In truth, he knew he hadn't had a choice in that matter. With grandma not allowing him access to his trust find until he turned 21 and graduated from college, he had been stuck in the Bahamas. Not that he blamed her, she did it for his own good, that he knew.

He was certain he had made the right decision, coming back home now, having found Susan again. He would start moving most of his business over here, to Florida, then he would only have to travel once or twice a year, and if things worked out, Susan could travel with him. He pulled up in the drive, jumped out and headed straight to his room to go to bed.

Andy wanted to get an early start on painting tomorrow. He wanted to get all of it done the next day, if possible, so he could get the carpet and then the furniture delivered as soon as possible.

Chapter Nine

THE NEXT MORNING Andy woke up early the sun was not even up. He fixed some coffee and ate him a bowl of oatmeal. When he was done he placed his dishes in the sink grabbed another cup of coffee and headed up to the top. He sat there drinking his coffee looking out in the ocean waiting to see the sunrise. As he waited for the sun to come up he started thinking of Susan wondering if she was up yet. He didn't ask her if she was coming today he just assumed she would because she said she would help. Heck he didn't even know if she was up yet. *I bet she sleeps until noon,* he thought laughing. As the sun rose over the water, the sky was painted with the most beautiful colors. Sometime he would have to make Susan get up early to watch it with him, although she probably already had since she'd been living by the ocean all her life. Well the time had come to get started, he was sure she would be there before too long. He decided to start painting upstairs, in the bedrooms, and work his way down. He started in the spare bedroom first, geez, what color had they decided for this room? He looked around for about thirty minutes before he found her chart listing everything they had decided on. He got the correct gallon of paint, a roller, a brush, and a ladder then headed upstairs. By the time he got it all taped off and started doing the trim, he heard Susan call out, "Andy, where are you? Are you here?"

"Yes! Come on up I'm in the spare bedroom"

"Okay, I brought us some extra help." Susan came flying into the room, "Sorry I'm a little late,

I wasn't sure what time you were going to start." Andy heard others coming up the stairs, so he grabbed Susan and stole a quick kiss, before whoever she had brought walked in. A young couple entered the room talking and laughing, when Susan interrupted, "Alright y'all, let me introduce you. Carol, Ned, this is Andy."

Andy said "Hi" and shook their hands.

Susan explained, "Carol is my best friend and Ned is her boyfriend. They were both off work today so I kind of recruited them to help us."

"Thanks Susan, I hate to take y'alls day off but we sure could use the help."

Carol and Ned replied, "No problem we haven't seen much of Susan lately and decided if we wanted to spend time with her, we would have to help."

Susan laughingly replied, "Y'all it hasn't been that long!"

"Oh yes it has, ever since Andy moved back, y'all are inseparable."

Susan responded, "He's only been here a few days and we are catching up, beside he wants my help."

"UM HUMM!", they replied at the say time laughing.

Susan blushed and Andy just laughed and said "Susan hun you just gave it all away with that pretty little blush you do." Then they all laughed. "Yeah, yeah, yeah," Susan laughed, "Just get to work."

Andy laughed all the way down the stairs after telling her he'd be right back with the paint and supplies for his room so they could get started. Ned and Carol had brought a radio and they had the music blasting through the house. With Carol, Ned, and Susan's help they got busy and by nightfall, they were all done. All that was left was cleaning the brushes. Andy thanked them and let them know how much he appreciated their help. They all grabbed cokes and headed out to the front porch to get some fresh air.

As the foursome walked out the door, Patty was heading up the steps with her hands full of food. "Hi y'all, I thought ya might be hungry."

"Man are we ever" Ned said, and the others all agreed they were starving.

Patty told them to have a seat while she got dinner out on the table, then they could each come get a plate. While they drank their cokes, Patty set out fried chicken, potato salad, baked beans, some rolls, and a pitcher of ice cold sweet tea. Patty called, "It's ready y'all, come and get it."

"Wow!" Andy said, "Patty, once again, you have out done yourself ." they all filled their

plates while Susan told her mom she shouldn't have gone to all this trouble.

Patty replied, "I had a little time on my hands, besides y'all were working so hard that you missed lunch. I knew you had to be hungry after working all day, besides, what are neighbors for."

Andy responded, "I'm sure glad you're my neighbor, but maybe you could be my girlfriend's mom too."

"Well now Susan, have you forgotten to tell me something?"

"Yes Mom, he asked me last night to be his steady and I said yes."

"Oh! I'm so happy for you, I just know you two are going to get along just fine."

"Now Mom, don't go rushing us we are going to take it slow."

"Okay, fine by me, that way y'all can make sure it's right."

After they finished eating Carol and Ned thanked Patty for the supper and headed home. Andy told them it was nice to meet them and thanks for all the help. Susan said "Wait and I will help you pack this all home."

Andy said, "No you are tired, I will walk both of you ladies home and pack it myself."

They headed on up the beach and Andy thanked Susan for all of her help that day. They discussed what all they had gotten done and how they hoped it would be dry enough tomorrow for them to get the carpet installed. When they arrived at the house, he told Susan goodnight and to get some rest, he would talk to her tomorrow. Susan told him goodnight before following her mother inside.

Susan headed straight to the bathroom to get in a warm tub of water to soak. After her bath she pulled on some pajamas and headed to the den to watch

TV. Andy walked back home he was really tired and he knew Susan was wore out. When he got home, he headed for a hot shower and then straight to bed.

Chapter Ten

ANDY WOKE UP around seven, not wanting to get up, but he needed to check and see if the paint was dry so he could call the flooring people to come out and do the floors. He was only putting rugs on the bedroom floors and then the hardwood floors throughout the house would be restored. He fixed himself some coffee and looked around, seeing the paint was dry, he decided to call them when they opened. After he had breakfast and got dress, he saw that it was time to make the call, they told him they could be there in a couple hours. He told them, he would be here. While he was waiting, he went up top and replaced the light, he knew Susan would be pleased with that.

When Susan got up, she was a little sore and moving slow. She couldn't believe how much work they had gotten done yesterday. She went downstairs to the kitchen and found her.

"Hi Mom."

"Good morning Susan, did you sleep well?"

Yes thank you, I didn't realize how tired I was."

"Yes, y'all worked pretty hard yesterday. Andy's working pretty quickly to get that place done. Do you know why he is in such a hurry?"

"No Mom, I just figured he wanted to make it livable, I mean, he said he plans on living there. I hadn't really thought about it much other than that."

I just don't want you getting your hopes up and getting hurt you take things slow and see where they lead, okay?"

"Okay Mom." Susan went upstairs to get dressed so she could go into town with her mom.

Andy was out on the porch when the flooring crew pulled up, he was so happy that the carpet would be down today and the rest of the floors redone. Then he could have the rest of the furniture and decorations delivered. That delivery would give him another excuse to have Susan over. Not that he needed an excuse, but he did want her input on how to arrange the furniture and where to hang the pictures. There's just certain things that women can do to make a house look like a home and he wanted a nice and cozy, inviting environment for anyone that came to visit. Andy was exhausted as he headed to the kitchen to make a sandwich and grab a coke to take up to the top so he could watch for ships and dolphins out on the ocean while he ate. As he gazed out at the horizon, he saw a few ships sailing past. It was starting to get dark and the last couple ships had noticed the new light shining brightly. He wondered if they were happy to have the beacon working again, A few of the ships sounded their air horns at the sight of the new, functional light. Their acknowledgement made him feel really encouraged and reminded him of when he was young again. He remembered being up here with his mom while his dad was down below unwinding and watching TV. After a while he got up to head down this was the first day since he had met Susan he hadn't seen her. Hum, I wonder what she has been doing today. He decided to take a shower and just head on the bed it was already after ten he didn't realize he had stayed up at the light so long. He was pretty tired he has worked hard for the last couple days and had another day like it tomorrow. So he took a shower and headed to bed it didn't take long to fall into a deep sleep.

Meanwhile, Susan went into town with her mom for a girl's day out. They had a good day of shopping and stopped for lunch before heading home. After they arrived home she helped her bring in their purchases and put them away. After her mom had gotten supper started, she told Susan that she could take off for a while. She had it started and under control so Susan was free to go out and have a little fun. Susan asked her mom if she was sure and let her know that she was going to go out to the beach for a little bit. On her way upstairs to change, she called Carol to see if she wanted to meet her out at the beach to hang out.

Carol said, "Sure, I'm not doing anything else, I'll meet you there."

Susan threw on one of her favorite bikinis, a light blue one, and grabbed a towel as she headed out the door. As she started across the back yard she saw Carol was already out on the beach.

"How did you beat me when I live on the beach?"

Carol laughed and saying, "You didn't ask where I was, when you called I was almost here hoping I could get you down here."

They laughed together as Susan spread her towel out before they took off towards the water. The girls splashed around and swam a bit, having a great time in the water before deciding to lay out for a while.

Carol joked, "I can't believe you're not with Andy."

Susan laughed replying, "Well you aren't with Ned either!"

"Come on Susan, what gives? You really seem to like him."

Susan smiled blushing, "Yes I do. Isn't he the most handsome man you have ever seen? Well, for you, it's Ned I guess. Anyway, I think Andy is the greatest! I'm so glad he's back, it seems like we almost picked up right where we left off. I mean we are still very comfortable around each other it's not like awkward or anything. It's really just like my best friend has moved back home." I mean as being comfortable "Hey! I thought I was your best friend," Carol cried in indignation!

"You know what I mean," replied Susan laughing.

"Yeah, I know y'all seem so right for each other."

It was getting late and Susan knew her mother would be calling her in soon, so they decided to call it a night.

"Want to stay for supper?"

"No thanks, I have a date with Ned."

"Ok then I will talk to you tomorrow."

Susan headed back up to her house reminiscing over the wonderfully relaxing day that she had had with her mother and her best friend. As she walked in the back door her mom said, "Perfect timing, supper is almost ready. Go on up and shower and change real quick so we can eat."

"Ok, Mom...umm did Andy call?"

"No, Sweetie. I'm sorry, he didn't, was he supposed to?"

"NO, not really, I just wondered. I'll be back down in a minute."

She rushed upstairs to take a quick shower and once back in her room, she didn't waste any time getting dressed, because she could smell the food all way up in her room. She hadn't realized how hungry she was. She headed to the dining room and found that her parents and Teddy were already there waiting on her. She apologized but her dad told her that she was fine as they had all just sat down. After supper with the family, she helped her mom clean up the kitchen and washed the dishes. When the dishes were done and the kitchen was all cleaned up, she told her parents goodnight and headed up to her bed.

Chapter Eleven

As Susan lay in her bed thoughts turned to Andy. She hoped that everything was okay since he didn't call her like he said he would. Oh well, he must have been busy. She wondered how much he had gotten accomplished today on the house. She decided she would walk down there tomorrow and see how much progress he was making. and if he needed any help. She didn't want to come on too strong, but she had missed him a little today. She tossed and turned because couldn't get comfortable. She had gotten a little too much sun today so her skin was tender and achy. As she finally drifted off to sleep her final coherent thoughts were of Andy and once again her dreams were filled with him.

The next morning, Susan found her mom sitting at the kitchen table drinking her morning coffee.

"Hi mom, do you have any plans for me today or do you need me for anything? If not, I was thinking of walking down to see Andy and check on his progress."

Patty laughed, "Well Susan, why don't you just say; Mom, I hope you don't need me today because I want to go to Andy's."

"Well do you?"

"No, sweetie I don't go ahead, after you have your breakfast."

"Ok thanks," she grabbed a bowl of cereal and sat at the table with her mom to eat a quick breakfast. As she finished she placed her bowl in the sink and headed out the back door calling out a goodbye to her mom.

Her mom waved goodbye and warned her not to be too late.

Andy got up, showered, and ate a bowl of oatmeal. After breakfast, he grabbed a cup of coffee and headed up to the top balcony to sit and watch the ships go by while he planned his day and waited for the furniture to be delivered. Sitting there looking out over the ocean and beach, he saw someone moving his way out of the corn of his eye. He stared wondering if it could be Susan coming to see him. He hadn't called her yesterday and he hoped she wasn't upset with him. As the figure got closer to the lighthouse, he could clearly see it was her. He stood up waved and called out to her and then started whistling to catch her attention.

Susan covered her eyes looking up and yelled, "Hi there stranger you didn't call me."

He apologized, "I'm sorry! I was so busy yesterday, we worked pretty late so we could get it ready for the furniture. In fact I was going to call you and see if you could come help me today, when it gets here. I'll meet you down stairs."

"No it's ok I will come up there, I love the view from the balcony."

"It really is a pretty great view, but you look even more beautiful."

She giggled on her way up to join him as she thought to herself, no one had ever told me I am beautiful before and I think I like it. Reaching the balcony, Andy was waiting for her.

"Oh yeah, my view just got even better. Nothing like a close-up," he pulled her into his arms, pulling her against his chest, before he lowered his head for a kiss. Their kiss started out slow but as he kissed her, she wrapped her arms tightly around his neck leaning into him. Andy moaned, breaking off the kiss to say, "Hun, you are killing me."

Susan giggled as he brought his head back down for another longing kiss. She slid her hands into his hair pulling him even closer as his tongue plunged into her mouth to dance with hers. As she whimpered with her desire, he lost it, pulling her down into his lap while never breaking their kiss. As they continued kissing, their desperation for each other grew to a near breaking point. Suddenly they were pulled apart when someone yelled up to them, "HEY! Got a truck load of stuff to deliver here. Do you want us to maybe come back, or think y'all can stop long enough to come down let us in."

They broke apart laughing and Andy called down, "I'll be right there!"

Susan jumped from his lap, blushing all the way to her toes. He laughed, "You stay her for a little bit, until your blush fades some."

She laughed smacking him on the arm, "It wouldn't be that way if you hadn't started
Something that you knew we couldn't finish this morning."

"Hun, I can't wait until we can finish it!"

Of course that's all it took for her to go beet red again. He went down to let the guys in and she thought back over their hello kiss. Wow he can kiss! She knew that she had better be careful if she didn't want to get too carried away with him. It was way too easy for her to lose herself in his kisses and his embrace. As she went downstairs , she saw that they were bringing in the couch. As the crew unloaded the furniture, she went with Andy to help him decide where it would fit best. After all the furniture was unloaded and in place, they unloaded all of the decorations, pictures, lamps and accessories. Andy told the guys to just set these items in the living room thinking that him and Susan would arrange them and hang the pictures.

After the delivery crew left he asked Susan if she would help him hang the pictures and arrange all of the accent pieces. She told him that she would love to and he asked where they should start.

"Might as well start here in the living room since that's where we are."

They took everything out of the boxes and spread it out around the room so they could decide where to put it all. After everything was sorted and put into their proper places, he thanked her for helping to turn his house into a home. The only thing still missing was the collage they had ordered from his family photos. He told her that they could run pick it up tomorrow and have lunch somewhere in town if she would like.

She gigled, "Are you asking me out sir?"

He laughed and said "I guess you could say that."

"Well okay then," she replied.

Andy looked up at the clock and saw that it was 2:00 pm already, he suggested, "Before we start hanging the artwork, let's grab a snack and head to the balcony to eat."

"Sounds good to me."

They went into the kitchen where he started grabbing stuff out of the refrigerator and piling it on the counter, he asked, "Mayonnaise or mustard."

She told him that he could pick, so he grabbed both. They ended up with turkey and cheese sandwiches, some fresh fruit, and a couple of cokes. They headed up to the balcony at the top and she noticed he had a small table and couple of chairs set up there.

"I didn't notice those before."

He laughed, saying "Well if memory severs me right we were kind of busy and you didn't look around much."

She laughed, "I believe you were the one who started it."

"Sure if that is how you want to remember things."

They sat at the new table eating and looking out at the ships passing by.

"I never get tired of this view," he remarked

"I don't either."

"I remembered it all those years I was away and just couldn't wait to get back to see it again. And now that I'm here there is an even more beautiful view that I hadn't really counted on."

Susan blushed, "I'm glad you came back too I missed you. But, we'd better get back to work or we won't get done before midnight."

Andy groaned, "Slave driver."

Laughing, they headed back inside to finish up their work for the day. They worked late into the evening so that they could get it all done. They finished up in his bedroom as had she saved that room for last, she was a little nervous about being in there alone with him. In here they decided to go with the light blue color on the wall and they had picked out a picture of a lighthouse beside the ocean. The lighthouse in the picture looked amazingly like his, then they went with some additional ocean pictures for a calming effect. They added in some small shell lamps that he had liked, for the night stands on either side of the bed. With the big dresser and mirror that took up one whole wall, that was pretty much it for his bedroom.

Susan suggested, "When we go into town tomorrow, we need to see if you can find a comforter and curtains for this room since you didn't find what you were looking for the other day."

"Okay, sounds good to me! We can just make it a whole day in town like we did before, if that's ok with you."

Sure I would love that. There are a few stores on down the road that we didn't go to. They are kind of expensive so I don't go there much."

"Okay, we will check them out tomorrow and see if we can find something we both like."

Susan sighed, "Well I'd better be heading home"

"I will walk you."

"Okay," they started down the beach to her home. As they crossed the back yard he told her he was sorry he hadn't called and was glad she came over today.

Susan replied, "I am too."

He pulled her into his arms and kissed her goodnight saying, "I'll pick you up at nine if that's okay?"

"Sure I'll be ready."

As Susan walked in the house, her mom said "I was just about to give up on you."

"Mom, I wasn't that late."

"Well come on, we were just about to sit down for supper."

After supper she helped her mom clean up then headed upstairs and went straight to bed. Andy walked back home thinking about how much they had gotten accomplished that day, and that week for that matter. He was thrilled that his house was coming together so well and that Susan was really leaving her imprint on the home. Unfortunately all this work had made him very tired. Arriving home, he sat down in the living room on his new couch and turned on the radio to unwind. While sitting there he found himself drifting off to sleep. Waking up a few hours later he turned the radio off and dragged himself up to bed.

Chapter Twelve

Andy picked Susan up at ten the next morning, as he walked up the front door to knock, Susan opened the door. "HI! I'm ready if you are."

He looked at her and said, "You sure are! You look so pretty."

"Thank you," she said looking down at what she had on, "but it's just a pair of shorts and a tank top."

Andy smiled, "Yeah, but what a pair of shorts and I love that top too," her shorts were a pair of old faded blue jean shorts she had cut off and that made them short shorts, then she had on a really tight pale yellow tank top cut really low. He told her, "I think I may have a heart attack before this day is over cause your killing me in that outfit." With her slender, long, tan legs ending in a pair of white sandals, and those legs that go on forever, he could almost picture that perfect little butt inside those short shorts. As he helped her into his truck, he thought he would pass out when he caught just a glimpse of her butt cheek peeping out from under her shorts. He smiled thinking that he was going to have to help her in and out of this truck as many times today as he could.

Susan settled onto the seat and watched Andy as he walked around the truck and climbed in. "What are you smiling about," she asked?

"Oh, nothing," he wasn't about to tell her what he had been thinking about, so he changed the subject as fast as he could. "Where do you want to go to first?"

"How about some of those antique stores I told you about, the ones that we didn't get to the other day."

Okay," and they headed off to town.

When they got to the first store, Andy said "you wait and let me help you down now I don't want you to fall and skin those pretty knees."

She smiled not knowing the real reason he was so eager to help her out of the truck. He opened the door and took her hand as she started to get out, she said, "Hang on a second, I think I have a rock in my sandal." She leaned over and pulled it out without knowing about the nice view she was giving Andy, looking down her top. It was a perfect peek of the two most beautiful, round breasts he had ever seen. She looked up at him, catching where his eyes were focused and blushed, pulling her shirt up a little. He smiled, "Oh hun, don't pull it up on my account that view is just about the prettiest thing I have ever seen." Susan blushed again as she took his hand and climbed down from the truck.

Andy pulled her into his arms as soon as her feet hit the pavement with a kiss so fierce, she almost lost her balance, her legs were suddenly jello. "See what you do to me hun?"

She gasped as he rubbed against her, "If you keep that up, I won't be able to stand up. You took my breath away with that kiss."

He whispered, "We could always go find a place for you to lie down and let me continue where I just left off."

"We had better not, we have to get the rest of the things you need for the house."

"Hun, right now, all I need is you."

They finally entered the store and a clerk came over to see if she could help them find anything. She completely overlooked Susan and started openly flirting with Andy. Andy smiled and told her they just wanted to look around, she said, "Okay sugar, but if you change your mind just let me know. My name is Cindy."

Giving Susan a look that could kill, she felt like she was one lucky lady as Cindy walked off. Susan giggled nervously, "I think I will wait in the truck, apparently you don't need me here when she can help you."

"No way, Darling, you're helping me. Besides I want your opinion, not hers. Not to mention, I just love watching your little shorts shimmy when you walk in front of me. She doesn't have any shorts on."

Susan knew he was loving the view so she decided to pick on him a bit, "I can go across the street and buy me a pair of pants if you don't like my shorts."

He laughed saying "No, no, no the shorts are just fine in every way."

Together, walking hand in hand, they looked around the store and picked a few things out for his home. Among their purchases were a couple of end tables for the living room with some really beautiful old lamps that would really set it off. They both thought these items would make the living room look great with all the colors they had incorporated. By the time they left this first store, it was lunch time so Andy asked her, "Where is a good place to eat?"

"There are a couple good places, depending on what type of food you want."

They talked about their options, and decided on a small café up the road. They went in and found a corner booth in the back with a view of the ocean. They looked at the menu and both decided to get a cheeseburger and fries. As they ate lunch, they discussed where to go next, he decided they could just pick the rest of what he needed at a department store and then go by and get the collage they had made up from the frame shop. As they got up to leave, Andy placed his hand on the small of her back to guide her out of the café. Susan thought that his hand was so warm her back felt like there were sparks zipping all over it everywhere he touched her.

Driving to the department store, Andy was thinking of how easygoing she was and how he would love for them to go the beach tomorrow. They deserved a day off to just play in the water and relax, so he asked Susan if she would you like to go to the beach tomorrow?

"Sure and I'll bring us a picnic lunch."

"Okay, but then I will take you out for a nice supper."

They went into the department store, where of course all of her friends had to say "hi" to them.

They picked out curtains and blinds before Susan picked out some sheer door panels to go on the French doors in Andy's bedroom. Andy questioned, "Susan aren't those a little see through?"

Susan laughed, "Yes but they are upstairs, and if you're not right in front of them, they will be fine."

"Okay, if you're sure…"

"I am."

They finished up there shopping then headed to the store to pick up the collage they had framed, they were both excited to see the finished product. They picked it up, both agreeing that it had turned out better than they expected it to. they both loved it. Once they got back to the lighthouse they packed everything inside as quick as they could, both of them were eager to get see collage up on the wall.

After they got it hung, they loved it even more with all the pictures they had picked out of Andy growing up and his parents. It made the place look more like a home. There was even a picture Andy had slipped in which she hadn't seen, one of her and Andy playing in the ocean, swimming around with the floats and slashing water on each other. They were both laughing.

Andy set up the end tables and she positioned the new lamps, everything looked perfect. By the time they finished hanging pictures and curtains it was dark. Susan remarked, "I guess I need to be going."

"I will walk you home."

As they got to her house he kissed her goodnight and asked what time she wanted to come down tomorrow for their picnic?

"I will be there by eleven."

"I can't wait to see you in a bikini," Andy confessed, "Goodnight, I will see you in the morning."

He started back down the beach and Susan walked inside he house, hearing her parents in the living room. She went to the door, "Hi Mom, hi Dad." They asked her to come on in and have a seat. They talked for a while and she told them about all that she and Andy had gotten done that day. Then she asked her mom about the plans they had made for the next day. Patty said that she was okay with their plans, but her dad said she had to come home and shower before they went out for dinner, he didn't want her to shower at his house. They all laughed at his concern and she reassured him that she wouldn't have showered at his house anyway.

Patty pulled her up, "Come on, let's fix supper and we will make enough for y'all to take for your picnic lunch tomorrow."

"Ok," said Susan, "But let's not go to a lot of trouble since we are going out for dinner. I thought we would just have a light lunch, plus we don't want anything heavy while we are swimming."

Patty thought for a moment, "Yes, that's true. So what were you thinking?"

"How about some cokes, cheese, crackers, bologna sandwiches, and some chips? Then maybe a couple of slices of your famous apple pie?"

"How did you know I made those today?"

"I saw the apples on the counter this morning so, I was really hoping you did."

"Good thing I made two of them!"

After supper Susan helped her mom clean up, then told her parents "goodnight" before she went up to take a bath. She knew that after today, her dreams would surely be filled with dreams of Andy.

Chapter Thirteen

THE NEXT MORNING Susan started down the beach towards Andy's house. As she got closer she saw he had already brought a blanket, two chairs and an umbrella down to the beach. He was sitting there watching her and looking very sexy this morning as she noticed his swim trunks, but he also had on a tee shirt. She waved and teased, "Hey, you're not gonna get any sun like that!"

He laughed. "I didn't want to get too much and I really don't want you to burn that pretty skin of yours." Andy watched her as she got closer and came up talking to him. He couldn't wait to see her in a bikini, but she had a wrap on over it right now. He bet she would look great. Susan set the small cooler down and told him she had just brought them a light lunch for later on, since they were going out tonight.

He responded, "Well I really want to take you to a nice restaurant, but you will have to pick where because I haven't been out enough to learn the places around here yet." He was sitting in one of the chairs, so she sat in the other one. They talked for a while he thought to himself I've got to get her out of that cover up! Finally, when he couldn't stand the suspense any longer, he told her, "let's go in."

She said agreed and he stood to take off his tee shirt. Susan caught her breath, he was so sexy with his six pack abs just a light golden brown smattering of hair on his chest. He made her think he should be a model. Andy teased her, "Well? Come on." She suddenly felt shy, wondering what had possessed her to choose this bikini today. There wasn't much to it, especially not for her top anyway, as she kind of spilled out over it. She had been very well blessed up top with a size DD. She never had any complaints from anyone else, oh well here goes.

Andy watched her slip out of her cover-up, not believing his eyes. He knew she was built, but oh my, she was built like a brick house. Very well endowed at the top with a waist so tiny, he bet he could place his hands around her and they would meet. She was just so tiny but her hips flared out just enough to let you know she was all woman. He couldn't speak as his Adams apple just bobbed. She had on a very light green bikini and the top barely covered her beautiful breasts, and her bottoms…WHEW! Well let's just say they'd make any man stand up! What there was of it, it was also light green with a small white ring on either side of her hips. Just when he thought that the view couldn't get any better, she turned and he saw her cute little butt, the bottom of the suit was a thong. Her whole little back side hung free and tanned, it was just the right size to grab a handful of it and hang on.

Susan noticed his slack-jawed stare, "What?"

Andy found his voice again, "My God Susan, you are gorgeous! I don't know if I want to swim or take you to bed right now! I sure hope no one else comes this far down the beach today, I'd hate to have to kill all the guys for looking at you in this bikini, when all I want to do is take it off of you."

Susan laughed, "Well we better go get in the water so you can cool down then."

"Ugh, you're killing me woman!"

They swam around ducking each other and playing around in the surf. Eventually they decided they needed to get out and dry off to put some sunscreen on. Andy noticed she was getting a little red. Susan teased, "Um Hum you just want an excuse to rub lotion on me"

"Darling, I want to do more than that to you right now." He let her get out of the water first so he could check out the view from behind.

She turned back, "Don't think I don't know what you're doing." He coughed, "Who? Me?" Suddenly he got all choked up as he noticed how she looked from the front. Where she was wet, she had tossed her hair back, and her breasts with those nipples… How he wished he could see them, they were puckered up just enough to stand out and make him take notice. He thought, Man I've got to do something before she sees what she's doing to me.so he dunked down again into the cool water, trying to think of something/anything else, while she grabbed her towel and wrapped up in it. She was sitting there drying off as Andy came up, he grabbed his towel and they sat under the umbrella talking and watching some kids play down the beach.

Susan joked, "Looks like you got your wish, there aren't many people out here today."

"Yeah, I'm glad, I'd hate to make you leave that on."

"No way, I wear this bikini a lot! How do you think I got this tan."

He groaned, "I don't like it that other guys have seen you in that."

She giggled, "Girls wear them all the time around here." She decided to give him a break and changed the subject, "Are you hungry yet?"

"Sure, if you are."

"Okay, let's eat," she unloaded the cooler passing out their lunches and they ate lunch while talking and relaxing. They threw a few crackers at the pelicans and watched them swoop down to get them. They both laughed when one of the birds got brave and took a cracker right out of Andy's hand. As they finished eating, Susan put all the stuff away so they could lie out for a while.

Susan asked Andy if he would like her to put some sunscreen on his back, "Yes, thank you, then I will return the favor for you. "Okay," she agreed. As she started rubbing his back, she could feel all his muscles flexing. She didn't think putting sunscreen on him would turn her on but it most definitely was. She noticed is muscles were relaxed until she got down next to the waist of his trunks and then his muscles got very taunt. She noticed, asking "Are you ok?"

He reassured her that he was ok, so she moved to the back of his legs. She started at the bottom and worked her way up she had gotten to the bottom of his trunks legs when he growled, "That's enough, now let me do you."

Susan giggled and laid face-down so he could put sunscreen on her. She smiled, thinking about how she had teased him while rubbing the lotion on him. Soon she realized what a mistake she had made in teasing him…

He started at her neck rubbing his way down to her bikini bottom, then he started again at her ankles moving upward with slow tantalizing strokes of his hands. Ever so lightly he stroked the inside of her thighs ever closer to her womanhood. She thought she was surely going to die from spontaneous combustion. She was biting her lip to keep from crying out in pleasure, his hands felt so good on her body. Suddenly, his hands were gone, he stopped, but only to put some more lotion on his hands. To her surprise, he started rubbing her bottom, no guy had ever touched her there let alone put sunscreen on her there. He rubbed from the top squeezing just a little as he went, knowing full well, the effect he was having on her. He could hear her sharp intake of breath and smiled to himself, and then his fingers reached the middle of her bottom, he dipped in between her legs rubbing very lightly. He could feel the heat radiating from her core and he knew that she was melting under his touch. What he hadn't counted on, was that while he was trying to pay her back for teasing him, it had backfired and now he was just as hot as he thought she was.

Slowly he bent down and kissed her neck, whispering in her ear, "Susan I want you so bad if I don't stop now, I'm going to end up making love to you right here on the beach."

Susan giggled and moaned, "I guess you better stop and lay down then."

He growled, laying down beside her. She smiled over at him, "Andy, no one has ever touched me like you just did."

Andy smiled at this knowledge, thinking he was glad there had been no one else for her. He said "Susan I want to show what it feels like to have a man make love to you, when you are ready."

She smiled asking, "What time are you picking me up tonight?"

He grinned knowing s he was changing the subject, "Will seven o'clock do?"

She smiled, "Yes, I will go home in a little bit to get cleaned up" Andy said he would too, then pick her up at her house. They discussed some places to go but then she told him after naming a few, he could decide. She gave him a selection with different kinds of food they served and told him she liked them all so he could pick. He laughed and said "ok".

They swam some more, then around five they decided to head home and get ready for their date, tonight he asked her if she wanted help carrying the cooler home but she said, "No, I'm fine, It's empty now. I will see you soon."

"Okay," he pulled her into his arms and gave her one hot kiss, as his hands roamed to her butt, she reached around and pulled them back up to her waist. He grinned, "Can't blame a guy for trying, after getting to look at that sweet little butt all day." Susan giggled, pulled on her cover up and headed off down the beach waving goodbye to him.

Chapter Fourteen

SUSAN WENT UPSTAIRS to take a shower and then decided to rest a bit before her date. As she lay down on her bed in her panties, bra, and robe, she quickly drifted off to sleep. She was awakened when Patty came in later, "Susan you better get up, its six fifteen and Andy will be here soon and you haven't even started getting ready."

"I'm sure glad I asked you to check on me."

"Yes, it seems that the sun got you good today. Sit up and let me put something on that burn you got."

"No Mom, wait till I get back home. I don't want to smell like Aloe Vera."

"Okay, well then, get up and get ready."

Susan got up and put on a pretty baby blue sundress with thin straps, it was cut very low in the front and was open in the back down to her waist where it flared out just a little bit to a short mini dress. Her dad hated it, but she planned to try and sneak out without him seeing it on her. She put on a simple pendant necklace and some dangling earrings that were simple. Surveying herself in the mirror, she thought her jewelry looked good and she decided to wear her hair up. Finally slipping on a pair of spike heels that made her legs look longer than they were and a quick spritz of her favorite perfume and she was ready to go. She hoped he liked the outfit that she has selected. She stood back and surveyed herself one last time, in the mirror, and thought, well, that's as good as it gets, I hope he likes the way I look tonight.

Andy drove up to her house dressed in a nice pair of navy blue dress pants and a white dress shirt, he wanted tonight to be special so he had called some of the places she had suggested and found one that sounded perfect, but it was more upscale, so he dressed for it. He knew she would look good, she always did, but the image of her in her bikini today, would be burned in his memory forever. God, she had looked so good, okay I have got to stop thinking like that, he couldn't get excited now. He didn't want to pick her up with a big ole bulge in his pants, that wasn't the impression he was going for tonight. He pulled up in front of her house and smiled with anticipation as he got out and walked up to the door. Susan saw him arrive from her bedroom window, so she headed down the stairs to meet him. She called out a quick goodbye to her parents and slipped out the door just as he was about to knock. He smiled as she stepped out onto the porch.

"My God you are gorgeous, I don't know if I should take you out or just steal you away to my house, you look good enough to eat! I'm convinced that you are trying to kill me before today is over."

"Thank you, you look pretty good yourself."

He took her by the arm, leading her down the steps to the truck. He helped her up into the truck and shut the door, then walked around and got in. He started up the engine and off they went. As they drove they made small talk, they talked about the things they passed on their way to the restaurant, the sights, as well as the things that they wanted to do in life. As they arrived at the restaurant, he told her to wait for him, he came around and helped her out of the truck. He wrapped his arms around her waist to lift her out, so she wrapped her arms around his neck and just slid down his body. Her body slid along his all the way down, until her feet rested on the pavement. As her feet touched the pavement her body was suddenly on fire, she had never felt like this before, everywhere their bodies touched she felt like a match had been stuck against her.

Meanwhile, he was consumed by his own thoughts and desires as she slid down the front of his body. He was wound tighter than a drum with wanting her. Never had a woman had this effect on him. He leaned into her and kissed her sweetly on the lips. He broke off the kiss and she let out a whimper as he moaned from deep within. He pulled away saying, "Oh Hun, if we don't get in there we are never going to eat."

Susan giggled as they walked into the restaurant. She was thinking about how he made her feel, it scared her a little, but he was so handsome and sinfully sexy. As they were escorted to their table all heads turned to take in the striking young couple. They were shown to a table in the far back with dim lights and a candle on the table. Andy helped her into her seat before he walked around and took his seat on the other side of the table. The waiter handed them their menus and Andy ordered their drinks. After the waiter left, she told Andy, "This place is beautiful, I must admit I have never been here, but I've always wanted to come."

"Well I'm happy to be the one who brought you here. This can be our place if we both like the food, because I have never been here either."

Susan noticed the dance floor just as the musicians started playing. Andy asked, "If you would like to dance, we can?"

"No, let's wait until after we have ordered our meals." Just then the waiter returned with their drinks and took their order. They both ordered lobster with a salad and they ordered a dessert to share, a chocolate mousse.

After they ate, Andy asked her once again, if she would like to dance and this time she said, "Yes." Taking her hand, he led her out onto the dance floor. There were only a few other couples on the dance floor as the next song started, it was a waltz which brought a smile to Andy's face. "This gives me a chance to hold you close like I have wanted to all day." She stepped into his arms willingly, as they danced she laid her head on his shoulder. He leaned down smiling and kissing her on her neck "Mmmmm you sure smell good."

She giggled, "Do I?" He sent shivers along her spine with his kisses and touch, that feels so good, she thought. She turned in his arms looking up into his eyes before she laid her head back on his shoulder, swaying with the music as he moved her along. She wished time would stand still as she loved being in his arms. He made her feel so special and she had never experienced anything like this before. She was pretty sure that she was falling in love with him and she wondered how he felt about her. She would not tell him how she felt, she wanted him to tell her first. She had always heard, if the man tells you first then they really do love you. She was going to wait this one out and see where it went. She didn't know how he felt, but she knew she was falling for him big time. They ended up dancing for quite a while, actually they nearly closed the place down. Andy took her arm and led her back out to his truck, he opened the door and helped her up into the seat. As they drove back home they talked about how much fun they had on the beach and how amazing their night had been.

    Andy told her he would love to take her out to do it all again sometime soon and Susan agreed. When they arrived back at her house, he parked in front and went around to help her out. He reached up for her and she slid down his body again, so close you couldn't put a pin between them. He groaned, "Hun, you're killing me! Do you know how much I want you and what this does to me?"

    Susan giggled as she held onto him. Keeping her body tight to his, she stood on her tippy toes and pulled his mouth to hers. As she kissed him, she didn't hold anything back. She slipped her tongue into his mouth and their tongues tangled in an age old dance, she sucked on the tip of his tongue and he groaned. Man, he thought, this lady could kiss him anytime. He decided to give her as good as he was getting as he changed the direction of their kiss, he kissed her hard and fierce, while letting his hands roam over her delicious body. He was so turned on and he pulled her even closer to him, grinding his body into hers, so she could feel exactly how turned on he was. She was getting so worked up, she felt him pull her closer and his hands were all over her. It felt like his hands were everywhere all at the same time. She felt the bulge in his pants when he pulled her to him and she moaned with desire.

Andy took her moans as a sign that she was as hot as he was, he slipped his hand into the top of her dress feeling her breast and seeking out her nipple. He rubbed it between his finger and thumb pulling on it gently until it puckered and she whimpered with desire. She broke the kiss sighing, "Andy we have to stop before someone sees us." Pulling away, he adjusted her dress again before he walked her up to the front door and told her, "Goodnight." They shared one last sweet kiss before she turned away and let herself into the house.

She went straight upstairs as it was late and she had told her parents not to wait up for her. Susan knew her parents were still awake as she passed their bedroom door because the light still shone from under it. She went into her room and got ready for bed, but she knew sleep wouldn't come easily tonight. Her heart was still racing as desire continued to pulse through her veins. She knew that when sleep did come tonight, she would only dream of Andy and their day together.

Meanwhile as Andy drove home he was thinking of Susan, she was so beautiful and full of life. They seemed to have a lot in common and he loved the way she could light up a room just by walking into it. He noticed how every head had turned her way at the restaurant tonight. Reaching his house, he grabbed a drink and headed upstairs to bed. As he drifted off to sleep, he was still thinking of her.

The next day Andy got up early and headed into town to run some errands. He needed to get a phone installed and he also needed to pick up a few more things he needed for the house. He went to the post office and mailed off some things and sent a letter off to his grandma. He needed to check on her and to see how she was doing, he hadn't talked to since her since he had arrived here and he knew she would be fit to be tied. She wouldn't think twice about letting him know it either. He arranged to have a phone line run and a phone installed the next week then he would call her and give her his number.

For now Andy would have to go to the only place he knew that had a computer in this town to email and fax some stuff to his offices over in the Bahamas. He planned on setting up an office here as soon as possible, that way he wouldn't have to travel near as much. He knew his grandma would have a fit when he did get his new office set up because he wouldn't be going over to visit her as often as she would like him too. He would have to deal with that when the time came, he had a good reason for not going back very much anymore, but grandma would fight him on it he knew. After he sorted through and replied to all of his emails and sent off the faxes, he headed to the café for some lunch. He had skipped breakfast in his rush to get his errands done, and now he was starving.

Walking into the café, he found a booth and seated himself, a young woman came over to take his order and poured him some coffee. He thanked her and enjoyed the view, looking out the window while he waited for his food. While he was eating, a couple of young guys came into the café. They were probably around Susan's age and he wondered if she knew them. They were talking among themselves but kept looking over at him every so often. Personally he thought that their staring was rude but he decided to ignore them. As he headed up to the cash register to pay, the waitress met him there. He gave her a nice tip and she smiled, thanking him and told him to be sure to come back. As he stepped out onto the sidewalk, he saw Susan and called out to her. She came over to join him and they started talking about their plans for the day.

He asked her if she wanted to go to the movies with him and she agreed. After the movie, he took her to a small diner by the ocean for a quick supper. When they finished he paid the waitress and she said she hoped they would come back. They both said they would, at the same time and laughed as they walked out the door. He took her hand, "It's such a warm night want to take a walk?"

"Sure lead the way," and off they went, they found their way down to the dock to get a closer look at the ships. They walked way out onto the pier to a bench where they could sit and enjoy the view. As they had walked, it had gotten dark and she couldn't believe she had spent this much time with Andy again today. It wasn't even planned, she just ran into him she was glad she had called her mom while at the movie to let her know where she was and that Andy would bring her home later.

As they sat down he put his arm around her, "This has been a very good night," he remarked.

Susan looked up at him dreamily saying "I think so too", she leaned against him and sighed, "This feels so right."

"I think so too." Andy tipped her chin up to meet his gentle kiss, "Susan, I think I'm starting to fall in love with you."

"Oh, that's good, I think, isn't it?"

He laughed nervously, "I guess that depends on how you look at it."

She looked up at him, confusion written across her face; he grinned and leaned down to kiss her. Susan wrapped her arms around his neck and leaned into him sighing. Feeling her surrender, he twisted her around and slipped his arm under her legs, pulling her over into his lap. She settled there, fitting so nicely against him. She adjusted her position, squirming a little to get situated, and maybe to tease him just a bit, he groaned.

"Darling if you don't stop your wiggling, I'm going to take you right here on this pier."

She giggled and melted into him for another kiss. He slipped his tongue inside her sweet mouth and she met his tongue thrust for thrust, their tongues mimicking a mating dance as old as time. Susan loved being in his arms, but sitting on his lap excited her as heat spread throughout her body and sparks of desire flooded her system. She could feel him growing with desire underneath her and it thrilled her that she could make him feel this way. Knowing that she could elicit this response in him made her giddy and imbued her with a sense of power as she realized that she was able to elicit such a response in him. Along with that sense of power, came a dose of nerves and a little bit of fear as well, she had never been with a man before and he was making her feel emotions and sensations like she had never experienced, he could make her lose her head with just a kiss.

Andy tore his lips from hers moaning, "Susan one of these days I'm afraid I won't be able to stop. We'd better head back to the truck so I can take you home, otherwise we'll end up spending all night out here. I want to take you right here and now!"

"Would that be so bad," she asked without thinking? Realizing what she had said brought a blush to her cheeks.

Andy laughed so hard at her embarrassment; he loved to see the blush rising on her face.

"What," she asked?

Trying to hold in his laughter, he exclaimed, "You are a little tease, and now, your game has got the best of me."

She jumped off his lap in indignation, "I am not a tease!"

He was still laughing when he got to his feet. He tried to pull her to him, but she jerked away angrily. "Oh come on Susan, I was just messing with ya. I'm sorry, you're not a tease, or at least you don't mean to be one."

"What does that mean," she huffed in anger?

"It means you don't realize how you affect me with all of your sweet kisses."

She blushed, "Well you started the kissing."

He laughed admitting his guilt, "Yeah, I did. But I can't help it. Your kisses are about the sweetest I have ever experienced. When I taste your lips on mine, I lose all control."

That did it, she flew back into his arms, he wrapped her up in his embrace and planted a quick kiss on her sweet lips. He pulled back and led her to his truck knowing that he had to get her home before he lost his fragile grasp on his self-control. He couldn't resist teasing her just a little more, "You're so cute when you get mad."

She punched him on the arm as he laughed at her aggravation. As they reached the truck she started to get in on her own and he gave her a playful little swat on the butt. She turned around to reprimand him when he shrugged, "I had to do something to get my hands on that cute butt of yours."

She smiled coyly, blowing him away when she suggested, "Why didn't you just ask?"

He laughed, more than a little shocked at her invitation, "Well then, alright, next time I will."

As her face turned a nice shade of beet red, he roared with laughter again. He walked around to get in the truck on his side. He drove her home, helping her down so he could get his hands on her one last time. At the front door, she stretched up on tip toes to give him a kiss goodnight. He pulled her into his arms as she moaned with desire. "You smell incredible," he murmured against her lips.

"Thank you and thank you for taking me to the movies and supper. I had an amazing time"

"You're very welcome. Now scoot or I won't be able to leave, then your dad will run me off."

Susan giggled at that thought and turned to head inside, blowing him a kiss over her shoulder as she closed the door.

She's going to be the death of me yet, Andy thought, shaking his head as he turned to leave. He wasn't sure about all of these new feeling he had building up inside of him, but he was anxious to see where they led. Never had he felt like this with any woman before. He headed home smiling and shaking his head as he thought back on their evening together.

Chapter Fifteen

For the next several days, Andy and Susan didn't see each other as he was busy trying to get his office set up and going in Florida. Susan took the time to visit and spend time with her best friends; Carol and Vickie. They met at the library to look over the acceptance letters they had each received from different colleges. They were all hoping to get into the same school so that they could room together. They had planned it all out, all that was left was to check their acceptance letters to see where they were all accepted to attend.

They were all so excited, but before the opened their letters, Susan told them all about Andy and how great he was. This was the first time Vickie had heard about him and she was really excited for Susan as this was her first real boyfriend. Oh sure, she had dated some before, but they were all jerks and she didn't keep them around very long. Once they were all caught up on what they had missed in each other's lives over the last week or so, they pulled out their stacks of letters.

As they sorted through all the letters, they found that all of them had been accepted to at least two of the same colleges. Now they had to check the course offerings to see which of the schools offered the majors that they were looking for. Carol wanted to be a nurse so she was happy when she found all of the classes she needed at one of the schools. Meanwhile, Vickie wanted to be an interior designer and eventually own her on company. Susan wasn't exactly sure what she wanted to do but she was leaning towards becoming a public account or a legal assistant. With these majors in mind, they were able to decide on one college that met all three of their needs.

Of course they all had to talk to their parents and see which college they would be able to go to. It wasn't much of a problem for Carol or Vickie, they had both earned scholarships, but Susan didn't quit have the grades and she just missed out on qualifying for aide, so she would have to see if her parents would be able to pay for her to continue her education. Maybe she could get a part time job to help cover her tuition costs. She had so wanted to go to college, but now after all the time she had spent with Andy she hated to leave him behind. Andy is a great guy and she would love to see where their relationship was leading, but could she throw away her plans and her dreams just to stay with him.

The girls had one more quick debate about which school they thought would be best for all of them. They agreed to talk to their parents this week and get back together next week and check on each other's progress. Leaving the library, they headed for the café to grab some burgers and milkshakes. After a quick lunch, they all head off to go their separate ways promising to call each other. The three young women were floating on the excitement and euphoria that comes from planning ones future.

Looking back over the past week, Andy couldn't believe he hadn't seen or even talked to Susan. He was busier than he had expected with getting his office set up. He had finally gotten his phone installed at home, but he couldn't find her parent's phone number as it wasn't in the phone book. Since their number was unlisted, he couldn't call her. She didn't how he even had a phone yet so she didn't call him either. He sure missed her and he wondered if she had missed him. He hoped that she had been thinking of him during their time apart. He decided to take a walk down the beach, as he wandered along the beach he was hoping to see her, but no such luck.

Giving up for now, Andy turned back towards the lighthouse and headed for home. He decided to just drop by her house the next day and ask her out for a date on Saturday night. He loved spending time with her and she had been such a tremendous help to him in fixing his home up. One thing was for sure, she had great taste and his house had definitely benefited from her feminine touch. The place looked amazing and was so welcoming and warm, he thought of his parents and wonder how they would like the changes he had made to their home. He hoped that they would have loved Susan as much as he was growing to and he wished they could see how she had grown into such a beautiful woman.

In moments like this, his pain felt fresh and the loss of his parents weighed heavy on him. Andy sure missed them right now, so he decided to reach out to his last connection to his parents, he picked up his phone to call his grandmother. He had missed hearing her voice and her constant support and love.

"Hello grandma, how are you?"

"Andy is that you? Well it's about dang time you called your old grandma! I was beginning to think your forgot me."

Andy laughed apologizing for neglecting her, "I am sorry, but I had to wait for them to get the phone line run and my phone installed. I have a phone number for you to write down so you can call me anytime."

"Good, good," she replied, "now what did I do with that pen? Let me find it then I can write it down." Andy smiled to himself; he could just picture her looking around for it. Picking up the phone grandma said, "Okay Andy, go ahead, I'm ready."

He gave her the number and asked how she had been doing and if she was taking her medicine. She assured him she was fine and was taking everything she needed, and then told him to stop worrying and tell her all about what he had been up to. After he caught her up he reassured her he would call again soon. She told him she missed him and loved him and to take care. He told her he would and that he loved her too then hung up the phone. Their talk had lifted him out of his melancholy and he was finally ready to get some rest.

Andy got up the next morning determined to ask Susan to join him for dinner this weekend. Pulling up he saw her mom working in the garden so walked around there to see how she was doing. Patty told him she was fine but that Susan wasn't here, so Andy gave Patty his new number and asked if she would give it to Susan. He told her he wanted to ask her out for dinner on Saturday night. Patty assured him she would give Susan the number and his message. He thanked her and told her to have a good day as he headed back to his truck. When he got home he had nothing better to do so he decided he might as well wash his truck so he gathered all of his car cleaning supplies together and proceeded to wash and clean it out. Just as he was heading back inside the clean up, his phone rang.

"Hi!" Susan said, "What cha doing?"

"Hi yourself! I just got done washing my truck and cleaning up some outside. How are you? I haven't seen you in a few days."

"I'm fine, I have just been busy with some work things," he explained, "but I have missed you"

"Thanks I have missed you too." Susan replied. "So you finally got your phone installed? Mom gave me the number and said you wanted me to call? I also put your number in my planner so I won't lose it."

"Good", he said, "I wanted to see if you would like to go out with me on Saturday night."

Susan thought for a minute about whether she already had plans before replying, "Sure, I would love too." She asked what he was planning for their date so she would know how to dress. He told her to dress casually and maybe, bring a swimsuit just in case. He hadn't finalized their plans yet, so he wasn't sure what all they would be doing.

She giggled nervously, "Ok, what time should I be ready?"

He told her he would pick her up around six o'clock pm.

"Well, I will see you then."

"Okay Hun, I will see you then." Well now that he had her commitment, he could start making plans for their date. He had an idea, but had to call to check on the availability and feasibility. He was excited about his idea and hoped she would like his plans. He wanted to give her an amazing night out to make up for neglecting her all week.

When Saturday finally arrived, he couldn't wait to pick Susan up. He was so nervous and he hoped she would like the plans he had made for them. Andy was wearing a pair of light weight khaki pants and a light blue polo shirt for their date tonight. He had been watching the clock all day and time had seemed to move at a crawl for him today. Arriving at Susan's promptly at six o'clock, he stepped up onto the front porch just as the door flew open. Apparently he wasn't the only one that was eager for their date. Susan stepped out onto the porch and flew into his arms.

"I'm so happy to see you," she said.

Andy laughed, "Me too, I mean, I'm happy to see you too!"

She giggled nervously, "Is this ok? I didn't know what to wear," twirling around for him to see her outfit.

She literally stole his breathe away, "Definitely!", he said, taking in every inch of her beautiful body. She had on a strapless sundress and he knew there was no way she had a bra on. He had noticed that right off as she threw herself into his arms, plus she had a little extra bounce in her breasts as she flew across the porch towards him. He liked her dress; it was shimmering pearl color that showed of her tan really well. She didn't have much jewelry on except for a pair of small ear rings that looked like little silver stars and silver flat sandals with the tiny straps around her ankles.

"You are one very sexy looking lady tonight," he told her. "Are you ready to go?"

"Yes," she replied and he led her off the porch towards his truck. As they walked to the truck, she asked. "Soooo, where are we going tonight?"

"You'll see, it's a surprise," he pulled over, into a marina and she looked at all the ships tied up there. "Come on, I think you're going to like this." He took her hand and led her up to a huge ship it almost looked like a yacht in fact it was probably a small one. Susan was in shock as they climbed aboard. The sun was just starting to set.

Susan noticed there was a table for two set with a chilled bottle of white grape juice. He led her to the table and pulled out her chair for her to sit. Just as she took her seat, music filled the evening air. She looked around and saw the three men standing of to the side with tuxedoes on playing.

"This is beautiful" she told Andy. She was in awe at all the trouble he had gone through for her.

He was thrilled that she liked everything so far. As he took his seat, the captain of the ship served then drinks and handed them a menu. He told them he would return in a moment.

Susan looked around, taking in their surroundings, the boat was a lot bigger than she had first thought. "Whose boat is this?"

Andy told her it belonged to a friend and he had borrowed it for the night. "Oh" she said, "It's really very lovely, quite beautiful, actually. I've never been on a yacht before,"

He told her he had hoped she would like it and enjoy herself. Just then, the captain came back to take their order. After supper Andy asked her to dance. Rising from the table they were both mesmerized, watching the most dazzling sun set either of them had ever seen. It was the most brilliant blending of colors as the sun dropped down until it look like it would just drop into the ocean. It was the most beautiful thing Susan had ever seen and she told him so.

"I'm looking at the most beautiful thing I have ever seen," Andy stated softly. Susan turned to see where he was looking and realized he was talking about her. She blushed as he pulled her into his arms to dance.

He noticed how, in the moonlight, her dress glimmered more as she moved. It was tantalizing. After a while they had stopped dancing and Andy snapped his fingers, the musicians disappeared along with the table and chairs. In their place was a huge chaise lounge. Andy led her over to the chaise where they sat and talked for a few moments before Andy started kissing her. The next thing she knew, she was in his arms and they were laying on the chaise kissing. She tilted her head a little as he moved down, planting kisses along her neck. Susan threw her head back and gasped as his mouth worked wonders on her awakening all of her senses.

She was hot; his hands were roving all over her at the same time as his mouth moved along her neck, leaving a trail of fire in its wake. He was kissing her neck as she moaned in pleasure arching her body into him, seeking a connection that she didn't quite understand. Andy was desperate to see and taste even more of her amazing body; her moans were driving him over the edge as she gave herself to him fully.

As they enjoyed the afterglow of their passionate encounter, Andy caressed her back, waiting for her to come down from her high. As she lifted her head, resting her chin on his chest, he asked, "Are you okay? Did I hurt you too much?"

A blush stole over her face as she found herself suddenly shy in her nakedness, "No you didn't hurt me too much, it was a little uncomfortable, but not too bad. Once we started moving, the pain was gone."

"It will be much better for you the next time. I didn't mean to hurt you but it's always a little painful the first time. I tried so hard to be gentle, but you made me lose control. I never want to hurt you."

"You didn't hurt me, it was perfect. Thank you for making my first time perfect." Susan sat up, feeling shy, she reached for her dress and pulled it on. As she finished dressing, Andy pulled his pants back on and made a call on the intercom, instructing the captain to head back into dock.

Turning back to Susan he told her that he didn't want their night to end, but it was getting late and he didn't want to get in trouble for being out all night. As the boat headed back to the marina, they lay on the chaise and cuddled. After docking he helped her up and kissed her before leading her back to the truck. Their drive back to her house was made in silence as the couple reflected on the events of the night.

At her house Andy told her how special she was to him and how much tonight meant to him as he kissed her goodnight. After returning his kiss and a whispered goodbye, Susan went inside and up to her room where she took a warm bath to clean herself off. She knew what to expect the first time so she had been prepared for it to hurt a little and for the discomfort she was experiencing now. After her soak in the tub, Susan slipped into her bed and drifted off to dream of Andy and the love that was growing between them.

Chapter Sixteen

As Andy arrived home, his phone was ringing, but by the time he reached it they had hung up. Oh well, he thought, if it's important, they'll call back. After giving his mystery caller a few minutes to call back, he headed up to bed. Sometime during the night he was awakened by a ringing in his ears, by the time he realized what it was, he had to race to make it to the phone before he missed the call again..

"Hello," he answered breathlessly.

"Hello, Is this Andy?" the woman on the other end of the line asked.

"Yes."

"Who is this?"

"My name is Abby; I'm a nurse at a hospital in the Bahamas. We admitted your grandmother here yesterday and she wanted us to call you since you are listed on her emergency contacts. Sir, you need to come as soon as you can, I'm afraid your grandmother is in pretty bad shape."

Andy hung the phone up stunned and terrified for his grandmother, he had just talked to her the other day she was fine. He jumped up, grabbed a shower and threw some stuff into a suitcase and headed to the marina to see when he could book passage back to the Bahamas. He was able to secure passage on a boat that would be leaving within the hour. He boarded the boat immediately and prayed that he could make it to her in time. Unfortunately, the journey to the Bahamas would take a few days, days that could make a difference between on time or too late. After three of the longest days of his life, Andy hailed a taxi and headed straight to the hospital, suitcase in tow. All the way to the hospital, he prayed that he would arrive in time to see his grandmother. Running through the hospital, he stepped up to the receptionist and gave them his grandmother's name, asking what floor she is on.

The receptionist checked on her computer before telling him, "Sir, if you will have a seat, her doctor will be out to see you soon."

Andy took a seat in the lobby and he waited and waited. Finally, a doctor came through the heavy doors to speak to him. The doctor stepped into the lobby and called his name. He said, "sir I'm sorry to have to inform you of this, but we lost her. Your grandmother passed away a few hours ago." Andy was stunned; his legs gave out as he sat down saying, "If only I could have gotten here sooner…"

The doctor said, "Sir, it was her heart. We couldn't do anything for her, it just wore out and she passed away in her sleep."

"Okay, I will have to make some arrangements," leaving the hospital, Andy headed for his grandmother's house. This was where he'd grown up over the last several years and he couldn't fathom the idea that his grandmother would never walk through the door again. He made several phone calls and took care of all the funeral arrangements. He suddenly realized that this was not going to be a quick trip; he was going to have to stay here for a few months, at least, to make arrangements and get everything taken care of. He would have to deal with her estate and her house would have to be sold along with all of the furnishings. It couldn't be helped, he had obligations here and he was going to take care of things for her the way he knew she took care of everything for him, his whole life. No matter how long it took, he had to do things up right, for her, she was the only family he had left after he lost his parents, she gave up her whole life to take care of him. After the sacrifices she had made for him, the least he could do was make sure he took care of things for her this one last time. If it took a few months, or a few years, it didn't matter as long as he did things right, and handled them as grandma would if she were still here with him. He just couldn't believe that she was gone.

Suddenly realization began to sink in and he was overwhelmed with grief. Self-doubt consumed him as he was suddenly wishing he had never left. If he had just stayed here, would she still be alive? For the first time since receiving the phone call on Saturday night, Andy let himself feel, he let himself have the breakdown that had been building for days. The memories of his life with his grandmother consumed him as he was suddenly pulled back to that time seven years ago, when his grandmother and he were forced to cope with the loss of his parents.

Grandma had been his rock, she was the only thing that had gotten him through the worst time in his life, and now she was gone. Now he had to learn how to go on without her. He had never felt so alone in his life, His world was officially upside down.

As the day of the funeral arrived, Andy wondered how he would ever get through this final goodbye, he didn't know if he was ready to accept that she was truly gone yet. He didn't know what to expect as he arrived for the service and he was pleasantly surprised by the crowd which had gathered there to honor her. There were so many people at her funeral who had loved and respected her, everyone present that day, considered his grandmother to be their friend. It hit him then how truly blessed she was. He shook hands or shared hugs with all of the people whose lives she had touched. The stories about his grandmother that her friends shared with him, would stay with him for as long as he lived. He realized now how blessed and enriched his life had been because she had been in it. She may be gone, but her legacy and her love with never leave him.

As the days passed, he began going through her house and sorting all of the stuff she had accumulated in her lifetime. It was a very emotional process sorting through her life and deciding what to get rid of. This was a long drawn out process because she never got rid of anything, ever.

Once he finished sorting through her personal effects, he would put the house up for sale and schedule an auction to sell the furniture and anything else that he wouldn't be keeping. The sorting process would likely take him a month or longer, so he was going to be spending a good deal of time in his former home.

While he was here he decided to make the arrangements to transfer the bulk of his business to Florida. While he would still have an office here in the Bahamas, he wanted his primary offices to be in Florida. He packed up the files and anything that he would need in Florida and made arrangements for these items to be shipped. Meanwhile, he also set about interviewing candidates to run his office here in the Bahamas. He wanted to hire a president to oversee the operations here as well, he was hoping that his current right hand man, Bruce, would be willing to accept that responsibility. Bruce had been with him since he opened his company and he knew that he could trust him completely. It was important that he establish strong leadership here so that he would be able to minimize the amount of time and the number of trips that he would have to make to just check-in. If Bruce agreed to take over, Andy would feel confident that when he left to go home, this office would be run exactly how it always had been. Andy also knew that he could trust Bruce to give the clients the service and help that they had grown accustomed to.

Chapter Seventeen

Back in Florida, where Andy had left in the middle of the night without telling anyone including Susan what was going on, she was growing angrier by the day. Of course she had no way of knowing what had happened to pull him away for so long and with no warning, or she may have not been so hurt. It had been over a week since their night on the boat. The night she had given him her everything, now she felt like a fool, he had played her good. He took her out he knew all the right things to say and do to get to her. He knew exactly what he wanted and stupid me, she thought, I let him have it. Stupid, stupid, stupid! She felt so betrayed for the first whole week he had been gone but she kept waiting for him to call. Finally, after a week of no contact, she walked down to the lighthouse and he was gone. By the second week, she had taken to hiding in her room, crying all the time, she was so depressed. She pulled herself together long enough to hang out with her two best friends; Carol and Vickie. They could tell right away, something was wrong.

"Susan," they said, "what's wrong you look terrible?"

"Gee, thanks," but she knew she looked awful, she had dark rings under her eyes; she had lost some weight and she hadn't been able to sleep much since

Andy had left. She told them all about the night on the boat. She even told them that they had made love, or at least she had thought they were making love, both girls knew it was her first time.

Carol said, "Susan I'm going to tell you something, you just forget about him. There are a lot of other guys out there, just mark him off and move on."

"But," Vickie asked, "Where is he?"

Susan sighed, "That is the most puzzling thing, he just disappeared in the middle of the night without so much as a warning."

Vickie suggest, "I tell you what let's search for him and when we find him I'll help you beat him to a pulp. I mean it too! Anyone who messes with my best friends. is messing with me." Jumping up she said, "Come on let's do some investigating and see if we can find anyone that knows where he is. I dare him to treat you like this." That brought a smile to her lips

Susan sighed, "No Vickie, sit down, while I appreciate you wanting to beat him up for me, this is something I just have to handle."

"Well, if you are sure… but, if you change your mind, we are here for you, Right Carol?"

Carol laughed and said, "We sure are, Susan."

They said, "Come on, you need chocolate, this is a good excuse for a piece of Chocolate pie."

The ladies all headed straight for the little café that was owned by a sweet old lady, named Nancy, in town. She had owned the café in town there for as long as the girls could remember. They always went there after school on Friday's to get a milkshake. She was known for having the best chocolate pies and milkshakes in the area. They walked in and Nancy said, "Hi girl's, y'all have a seat and I'll be right there." They picked a booth in the corner by the window and Susan kept looking out the window hoping to see Andy. She just couldn't understand why he had left, she told them.

Vickie said, "Girl, he led you on, he got what he wanted and now he's done."

"That's right," Carol said, "I hate to say it Susan, but Vickie is right. They like the chase and once they get it, they're gone."

Susan replied, "But Carol, you and Ned are still together and I know you said y'all have done it."

Carol laughed, "Yeah that's right, because I told him if he pulled that crap on me I'd cut it off sometime in his sleep."

They all laughed and Nancy came up to them asking, "Ok girls what's going on??? What will ya have??"

The girls each ordered a slice of chocolate pie and a coke.

Nancy said "Uh oh, chocolate, who has man trouble??"

Carol and Vickie both pointed at the same time, to Susan. Susan responded, "Gee thanks."

Nancy turned her attention to Susan and said, "Come on now Susan, tell Nancy all about it, then I will decide if I need to get out my shotgun."

They all laughed as Susan told her, "That won't be necessary, he left, just took off with no warning and I don't even know if or when he will be back."

"Well good riddance! If he can't see how special you are, then he isn't worth having. Now you just stop worrying over that young man and start looking at all the others."

Vickie and Carol laughed and said, "Yeah Susan, just wait until we get to college. There will be a lot more men to pick from."

Nancy worriedly asked, "Oh my, are y'all going to leave us this fall?"

They all answered together saying. "Yes."

"Well I'll be! Don't that just beat all? Seems like yesterday y'all were just little things going off to first grade. Okay, I'll be right back with your pie."

As Nancy walked away, the girls turned their discussion to college, Susan said, "I can't wait to get out of here and away from these memories, maybe that will help."

"I'm sure it will" Carol said "after all we will be so busy you will hardly have time to even think of that jerk."

"That's right," Vickie said, "We are going to party, well maybe, part of the time anyway."

Susan laughed at them watching Nancy return with their pie and cokes.

"You girls have fun now, be sure you come by and see me when y'all are home on breaks and I'll give ya pie and milkshakes."

"You got a deal," they responded in unison.

"Okay, good then I will see y'all later."

The girls ate their pie and started making plans for when they got to their new school. About that time, the door opened and in walked four guys the girls had gone to school with; Jake, Bill, Charlie, and Steve. They were all football players in high school, in other words, handsome jocks. They came in laughing and headed to a nearby table completely ignoring their presence, as always. The girls didn't care anymore though; they were out of high school now and getting ready to head off to college. They agreed right then and there, it was their loss. As if Charlie could hear their thoughts, he turned around, looked right at Susan, and winked.

"Oh! Did you see that," Vickie asked Carol?

"What?"

"Charlie just winked at Susan!"

Susan turned beet red and giggled, they both spoke at the same time saying, "Girl, what have you been hiding?"

"Nothing honest," she said but she couldn't stop giggling so her friends were not convinced. They decided to let it go as got up to leave the café. The girls filed up to the cash register to pay their bills. They walked right beside the table with the guys, a little too close for Susan's comfort. Just as she went past, Charlie whistled at her real low, she smiled but kept walking.

The other guys were being their normal, loud, obnoxious selves and didn't even notice the exchange. After the girls were outside on the sidewalk, Carol and Vickie started teasing Susan, something awful. They walked off down the street laughing as their conversation returned once again to college.

Since the girls would all be going to the same school they were planning to leave a month ahead of time to find an apartment and learn their way around campus. When they pitched this idea to their parents they ran into trouble. Their parents did not want them leaving that early, but finally Carol's mom volunteered to go with them to help find an apartment and get situated. She reassured the other parents that she wouldn't leave until she knew for sure the girls were all set and knew their way around the town. She would make especially sure they all knew how to get back home. After Carol's mother saved the day, the other parents agreed with their plans. The girls were going shopping to pick up a few things to take with them, but the most part, they would get whatever they needed after they found a place to live. It was just too hard to pick out stuff for a place they hadn't even seen yet.

As the weeks passed the girls grew more anxious to get started on their next great adventure. Finally the day had arrived, Susan was so glad to be getting away, she couldn't believe Andy still wasn't back, he hadn't even written or called.

Carol and Vickie pleaded with Susan to move on, "He is just a loser! Forget about him and think of all the guys we are going to meet in college."

Despite her friends' pleas and attempts at distracting her, Susan had a really hard time forgetting about Andy. She doubted she would ever be able to forget him; after all he was her first real boyfriend and her first love. The pain of knowing that he had taken advantage of her trust and her feelings for him broke something inside her. She wouldn't ever allow herself to be fooled like that again. It would be a very long time before she trusted anyone else with her heart, besides how could she give something away that she didn't even have. She wouldn't admit it to her friends, but when Andy had disappeared, he had taken her heart with him. Until she knew what had actually happened, she didn't know if she could truly move on with her life. Today was a new start though; she was taking the first steps towards starting over. Stealing one more look towards the lighthouse, Susan sent up a silent prayer for Andy, hoping that he was safe wherever he was. As she turned back to load her belongings in the car, she whispered a final, "Goodbye," to the only man she'd ever loved.

The girls loaded up the two cars they were taking with them. One of the cars would stay with them at school, so they would have transportation to come home and get around their new town. The other car was Carol's mom's car, which she would need to get back home once the girls were all settle in. The girls each said their "Goodbye's" to their families and piled into the cars. They had a long drive ahead of them. By the time they finally got into their new hometown, it was quite late. They pulled into the first motel they found and booked a room for the night.

The next morning the group went straight to the college campus to look around; from there they picked up a newspaper and started looking for apartments. They circled the ones that were within their budget and then made a list of the ones that they wanted to see. The girls made phone calls to all of the ones on their list, writing down directions and prices they set up several appointments to go look at the apartments. After three days of looking at apartment after apartment the girls were growing discouraged and were just about ready to give up. The apartments they had looked at were either too expensive, just plain nasty, or infested with bugs. There was one apartment left on the list, and they were on their way to see it now. They were all feeling pretty pessimistic after the encounters they had thus far, but they agreed to give it one more shot. The last apartment was perfect! They all loved it including Carol's mom and they signed a lease on the spot. Now they had to find some cheap furniture to turn this empty space into a home.

The girls' parents had all pitched in, giving them enough money to get some used furniture and new mattresses once they found a place. It took the girls about three weeks to set up their new home and learn their way around campus and town, but finally the time had come for Carol's mom to head back home. Her mom had made sure that each of the girls was comfortable finding their way both around town and to the interstate to get back home for school breaks. The girls each thanked Carol's mom for all of her help and said their, "Goodbyes". Alone in their apartment, the girls had a party to celebrate their independence. They rented some movies and cooked a feast for the three of them. It felt great for them to be on their own finally. The girls stayed up until 3 o'clock a.m. despite the fact that they had to be up the next day to go to campus. They got up early that morning and headed to the campus, they decided to go over and see if they could pick up their schedules. Once they got their schedules they could find all of their classes and the cafeteria.

As the girls made their way around campus they ran into a few guys' who were checking them out, if the catcalls and whistles were any indication, they liked what they saw. The girls giggled and continued on their way, knowing suddenly that this was going to be a fun year. On the way back to their apartment, the girls discussed the idea of getting part time jobs. If they were working, they wouldn't have to be so dependent on their parents for money all the time and it would give them the freedom they really wanted. They drove to the supermarket to pick up a few groceries and a newspaper to help them with their job search. They picked up a pizza for dinner on their way home since they all agreed they needed a break from cooking after the feast they had prepared the night before. After an informal supper of pizza and coke, they pulled out the newspaper over it together looking for part-time jobs close to the college. They also decided to check the bulletin board on campus to see if there were any part times jobs on campus. The girls didn't think they would have much luck with on campus jobs as they assumed most of those would probably go to upperclassmen first.

 The girls each found a few prospects that interested them and decided they all needed to put in for each of the jobs so if one didn't get it, maybe another one would and they also agreed that there would be no hard feelings. The next day they ate breakfast and headed out to look for part time jobs. That afternoon they each had orientations to go to for their classes. Since they were each pursuing a different major, they did not share any classes, so when on campus they would all be going in different ways. The girls wished each other luck and headed off to start their college careers.

 Within a couple of weeks things were settling down for the friends, they had established a routine at home and they were doing well in their classes. Through their classes, they had met a lot of new friends. Carol and Susan had found part times jobs while Vickie was still searching. On one particular day she got lucky and just sort of walked right into a job. She overheard a lady in the office at the school mention the bookstore needed some part-time help. Leaving the office, she headed right over to the bookstore to apply. She was the first one to apply for the position as they hadn't yet posted the opening. They agreed to let her have the job, it would save them from having to post the position and conduct interviews. She couldn't wait to get home and tell the other girls all about it. She rushed through the door and was assailed by the most wonderful smells. None of them had known, not even Susan had realized it herself, but she really had a knack for cooking. Tonight she had grilled pork chops, tossed a salad, and mixed up fried rice. Dinner had just finished cooking as she walked in. Carol laughed telling Susan, "I told you she would smell it." It was a delicious meal, after dinner Vickie told her best friends about her new job. The friends were very excited for her and Susan pointed out the practical advantages of Vickie's new job. "The best part is, we can have you pick up all of our books and save us the hassle of having to stand in line and fight the crowds."

The girls shared a good laugh over Susan's logic before they settled in for a movie. They talked about what they were learning in their courses. The girls had been in college for two weeks now and their classes were really starting to get interesting, but the teachers were also beginning to pile on the homework.

Chapter Eighteen

Between the responsibilities each one had; their jobs, courses and homework, the best friends soon learned they didn't have a lot of free time. Their own interactions happened mostly at night or in passing between school and work. Finally after a month of hard work, the girls all managed to get a Saturday night free and they were going to take advantage of the night off. They had all been invited to a party on campus so they decided to go, and maybe they would meet some more people, hopefully some cute guys, thought Vickie.

Luck was shining down on Vickie that night; there weren't just a lot of guy's, there were some really hot hunks there too. Susan had been talking to a few girls she met at the party, they were really nice and she had classes with some of them. They agreed to hang out another time as Susan's attention was pulled away from the ladies. Susan was looking across the room to a crowd of guy's that were being quite loud. Her eyes were drawn to one really hot, hunky guy who was looking her way. He caught her gaze as she stared at him and she turned back to her new friends while a blush made its way across her face. One of the ladies noticed who she was looking at and giggled warning, "Oh Susan, you better watch out, that one is a real ladies man. He's the love 'em and leave 'em kind."

Susan blushed and laughed, "Don't worry I got burned by that sort of guy this past summer I'm not even remotely interested in that game."

They all laughed with relief when one of the girls told her, "Well you better watch out then, because he has his eye on you. When he sets his mind on a girl he'll pull out all the stops until he gets her."

Susan remarked laughingly, "Well he doesn't know how stubborn I can be!" She was laughing on the outside, but inside she was admiring him in the same way he admired her, thinking what could a little fun hurt. Besides, she was in college and that was one thing college was about. He could only hurt her if she let him into her heart, but what could a little no strings fun hurt? With that thought in mind she committed to relax and have fun. She continued to watch him out of the corner of her eye all night and would catch him checking her out periodically as well. He walked over to one of the girls she had been talking to earlier and started talking to her so she shrugged it off figuring oh well maybe he isn't as interested in me as they thought he was.

Little did she know how wrong she was? She found out later he was over there asking all kinds of questions about her. Later on that night, as she, Carol and Vickie were preparing to leave the party, he walked up to her and introduced himself, "Hi, my name is Tony and I was wondering if you would like to go out sometime so we could get to know each other and all."

Susan smiled, "Thank you, but I don't even know you and I don't date people until I get to know them."

Now Tony wasn't going to let that discourage him he smiled, "I can't say as I blame you, how about we meet at a public place of your choice."

"Ok," she agreed, "How about we meet at the little fish place in town?"

"Cool, how's lunch, tomorrow around noon sound?"

Susan agreed, "Okay, see you then."

On the way home from the party, she soon discovered that she wasn't the only one to get asked out that night, Carol and Vickie had similar dates lined up for the next day. This was one thing the friends all agreed on, never trust a guy they didn't know, so they all set up dates in public places until they got to know the guys. Arriving home, the women were all worn out from the party and had big plans for the next day, so they went in and got ready for bed.

Time flew by for the girls between classes, working, and dating; before they knew it Thanksgiving Break had arrived. Carol and Vickie were heading home for break but Susan had talked to her mom, she had to work and couldn't get off so she was going to stay behind. While her mom was not happy, she told her she understood and made her promise to come home for Christmas break. Susan promised she would come home then. She told her mother that she missed her and loved her before hanging up the phone. Carol and Vickie tried one last time to talk her into coming along anyway but she told them she had to work and had a big test she needed to study for. With that, the girls gave up and headed home.

The next few days flew by for Susan, but it was the nights she struggled with, she felt so alone in the apartment. It had been a long time since Susan had experienced a sense of loneliness such as what she was going through right now. Not since Andy's disappearance had Susan felt so alone, With nothing else to occupy her thoughts, she found herself wondering whether Andy was back home, in the lighthouse. Susan realized that she was headed down a path she wasn't ready to be on, a path that her amazing best friends had rescued her from just a few short months ago. She told herself that she would not think about him, she refused to let him break her spirit. Seeking an escape from the solitude, Susan headed to the local pizza place for dinner. While she was there waiting to pick up her pizza she ran in to Tony again. She had gone out with him and she found out what the other girls had told her about him was true, he never gave up. He was a really nice guy and she found she really enjoyed spending time with him. He came up to her saying, "Hi Sweetie, how ya doing? I haven't seen you in a while."

"Hi Tony," Susan replied, "I'm good; I've just been really busy between work and classes."

"Yeah, I know what you mean and finals are not long off."

Susan asked, "Have you had supper, Tony?"

"No, not yet, I was just fixing to place my order."

"Well I called one in, how about coming over and helping me eat it? Maybe we can watch a movie?"

"You sure?"

"Yeah, it'll be fun, come on, I might even let you pick out the movie"

"Well alright then, I'll follow you to your place?"

"Okay."

Tony insisted, "I'll pay, since you asked me at the last minute. I feel like I put you on the spot." Susan smiled and his heart stopped. Wow she is stunning he thought.

"Okay, but for the record, you didn't have to pay. Come on lets go."

Following Susan home, Tony couldn't believe his luck running into her, and then she asked him to come over! Never before had she even invited him in. Maybe, he thought, she liked him a little more than he first thought. He was going to take things slow with her, he could tell she was shy and he didn't want to rush her or scare her off. It had taken him a long time just to get here to the point where she seemed comfortable with him.

They arrived at her place, he knew she had roommates, but when he went inside they weren't there. It appeared they would have the house to themselves.

He asked, "Where are your friends?"

"They went home for break, but I had to work so I stayed here."

"I bet your parents didn't like that, did they?"

"No, but they understood," She said, "What about you? Why didn't you go home?"

"My folks are out of town so I just stuck around here."

Susan thought that was odd, but didn't say anything. She was just happy she had run into him so she could ask him over. She walked into the kitchen, as he followed she told him to get the glasses down for her, telling him where to find them while she grabbed the plates. She dished out the pizza and poured their drinks and they headed into the living room to sit on the couch. She told him the list of movies they had then he picked one for them to watch, she said she liked it too so they popped in the movie and ate their supper. When they were finished eating, Tony took the plates and glasses back into the kitchen for her then came back to sit by her to watch the rest of the movie. He scooted closer to her and slipped his arm around her and she snuggled in close beside him. Tony thought, man, she feels really nice and smells good too.

Susan noticed when he had slipped his arm around her so she slid in closer beside him and leaned on him, he felt so good. It was so easy for her to relax around him and he was so nice. Those girls were so wrong about him. He had been a perfect gentleman around her and she was glad because she really liked him. He reached over, tipping her chin up, he leaned in to give her a kiss and what a kiss it was! Susan had to admit he definitely knew how to kiss. She could kiss him all night long. Wow, where had that thought come from? She liked him well enough, but no way was she ready for a physical relationship again; she hoped he didn't get that idea when she invited him over. He felt her stiffen a little in his arms and knew she was thinking about something else, he told her to relax because nothing would happen if she didn't want it too.

Sensing that Tony knew what she was thinking, she relaxed and they spent the rest of the movie kissing and holding each other. When the movie was over it was after 11 o'clock p.m. so Tony told her he had better get going. He didn't want her to think he expected something from her. It would be nice, he admitted, but no way was he going to push her. He realized tonight that he could grow to care about her, he loved spending time with her, and she was really easy to talk to. He could be himself around her and he liked that. The last two days of Thanksgiving break flew by and she found herself spending time with Tony whenever she wasn't working.

On Sunday, Carol and Vickie came back and they walked in on Susan and Tony all snuggled up on the couch kissing. Exchanging mischievous looks, the girls let out a loud, "Whoo whee! Now we know why you didn't want to leave." Susan jumped and Tony actually turned beet red at her roommates' comments.

Susan said, "No it wasn't that, but I did find some time to myself and Tony kept me from being lonely."

"Umm hum, what else did he help you find?" They asked while laughing.

Tony told Susan, "I better be going so you can have a chance to catch up." She walked him to the door and he told her he would call her later.

Susan turned around to find them staring at her with their arms crossed and tapping their feet.

Carol said, "Okay out with it."

Susan retorted, "Out with what? We were just watching a movie"

"Sure you were," Vickie said laughing.

They all sat together and Susan filled them in on what she had been doing. Carol and Vickie then filled her in on everything back at home including the fact that Andy was still not back. While Susan was happy to hear news about everything back home, she missed her mom something awful, she was really homesick now after listening to them talk about everything back home. She decided to go her room and call her mom and tell her how much she missed them and how sorry she was for not coming home. She told the girls goodnight then went to call her mom. After her call home she was so depressed she fell asleep while crying and decided right then she would go home every chance she got.

It seemed like only a few days had passed since Thanksgiving, but here it was almost Christmas break time for the girls. Susan was so excited, she couldn't wait to get home she had been dating Tony a lot lately; they had even been studying together for their upcoming finals. He was a great study partner, he was very smart and he helped her a lot. She felt very close to him, and of course after each study session they always took some time for a little kissing and cuddling.

On this particular day she ask him if he was going home for Christmas break she knew he didn't go home for Thanksgiving break and he never talked about his family so she didn't think he was very close to them. Unlike her, she was very close to her family and if he wasn't going home she was going to call her mom to see if she would mind if he came home with her. She knew she wouldn't mind, they always had a huge Christmas party anyway so what would one more person be. She asked Tony to excuse her real quick and asked him to wait for her, she would be right back. After she called her mom and told her the situation, her mom was more than happy for her to invite him. She told her it was about time for the family to meet him if she was involved with him and from what Carol and Vickie had told her when they came home she knew she was dating him.

Susan laughed, and said "now Mom, don't go getting any ideas we are just dating and having a good time.

Patty told her to, "bring him; there is always room for one more."

Susan came back to the table where Tony sat waiting for her; after she sat down and they talked for a few minutes she asked him again, "Tony, are you going home to be with your family for Christmas?"

Tony looked down at his feet and then back at her all flustered, he said, "No, my mom and dad are going on a cruise for Christmas, so I'm going to stay here. Don't you worry about me though, I will be fine."

"Oh no you won't! You're going home with me for Christmas."

"What?", Tony asked, "I can't, that is family time."

"Yes, you can. My family has a huge party every year at Christmas and one more person won't make a difference, besides I already called Mom she is looking forward to meeting you."

Tony's smile could have lit up a room, "Well ok then I guess I can come if you're sure."

"I am"

Tony suddenly realized what he had gotten into. Meeting the parents, Oh no, am I ready for that?

Is that what she was thinking? But it would give him somewhere to be and he really didn't want to spend it here at college alone. He would go and if she thought that she was ready to become more serious, then they would just talk it over, he thought a lot of Susan anyway but was he ready for that?

Chapter Nineteen

Andy couldn't believe how long all this was taking, settling his grandmother's estate after she had passed away. He had run into more problems than he ever could have predicted or expected. One thing was for sure, he had everything in order for establishing his business in Florida.

He had hired a skeleton crew, the ones who wanted to relocate had been hired for the Florida office, they were already there getting everything set up for him. He was going to be so happy to get back there to his home. He just had to break the news to Amy, since he had been back over here, she had found him and tried her very best to get him to take her back. She was a lovely woman, but she just wasn't right for him. Too high maintenance for him he thought as he laughed. He preferred someone like Susan. He couldn't wait to see her again; he bet she would be a little pissed since he had been gone so long. The way it was going he would be there by Christmas Eve, or maybe the day before. That was his plan anyway; he couldn't wait to get back home. It would be a nice surprise getting there in time for Christmas. He would take her a gift to try smooth over since she might be mad. He was going to say all of his goodbyes here today and he hoped to be able to leave within the week. The next few days flew by for Andy, but now he was finally on his way back to his new home, his forever home, the lighthouse.

Andy got back to the lighthouse, finally, it had been a long trip and he was so glad to be home. It was late, so he went straight up, showered, and went to bed. He knew he would have to clean out the refrigerator and go to the grocery store to restock. Right now, he was exhausted; he got out of the shower and headed straight to bed. The next day Andy drove to town thinking he would have to swing by and see Susan today. He would surprise her, it was 3 days before Christmas and he had a lot to dodo.

He would be spending his first Christmas here at the lighthouse and suddenly he realized he would be all alone. His parents had been gone awhile but still he missed them at this time of year; and now with grandma gone too, it was going to be really hard this year. She had always been there for him and he would miss her so much. He got in to town around 10 o'clock a.m. and he got all of his errands done and headed back home around 1 o'clock p.m. By the time he got all of his stuff done, he decided to walk down to Susan's. As he walked across her backyard he noticed they had put their Christmas tree up and it looked so pretty. He knocked on the back door and Patty came to answer.

"Well, hello stranger! Where have you been? We haven't seen much of you lately…"

- Andy smiled and told her all that had happened to keep him away. He told her about the death of his grandmother and the difficulties with closing out he estate and transferring his business interests to Florida.

"I'm awful sorry to hear about your grandmother."

"Is Susan here?"

"No Andy, she has been gone since August."

He looked at her in confusion so she explained, "She is in college now, she will be home soon for Christmas break though, in fact, we are having a party on Christmas Eve if you would like to come."

"Okay, if you are sure it's okay?"

"It's fine, I think you and her need to talk, although she is pretty upset with you."

He assured Patty that he would talk to Susan and straighten things out.

"Good, so we'll see you then."

As he walked back down the beach, he couldn't believe she was gone he didn't even know she was thinking of going off to college. He just assumed she would go to the community college here. Well, at least she would be home soon and he could straighten things out with her and see where things stood with them. He walked on back home and going inside, he decided to go get him a small tree and maybe Susan would help him decorate it when she got home.

He couldn't wait to see her.

After driving around, he finally found a lot with a few trees left; he stopped and picked out one he thought would look ok. He paid for it and headed home. The next few days drug by for him he was so excited to see Susan. He decided he needed to do something to make his time to go by faster, so he went to work and filled his days and most of his nights with working. Finally it was Christmas Eve and the party at Susan's house was tonight. He was wearing a pair of his black dress pants with a light blue dress shirt.

He drove up the road toward the house and there were cars parked everywhere. He found a place to park and went to the door. Patty answered the door, inviting him in. "Andy, Welcome! I am so happy that you could make it tonight. Please make yourself at home; the food and drinks are in the dining room."

He asked, "Is Susan here yet?"

"Yes, she is around here somewhere."

Andy walked off in search of Susan, making his way around each room talking to the few people he knew among the guests. Suddenly, he saw Susan from across the room. She looked beautiful as always. She hadn't seen him yet; just as he started to cross the room to speak to her a guy walked up to her and put his arm around her. She leaned into him and he kissed her. Andy felt like he had just been punched in the gut. Who the heck was he and why was she with him? He thought for sure they had something special, what had gone wrong? He needed a drink so he turned and went into the dining room to find some fortification. He was in the dining room talking, laughing and drinking with a few friends when Susan walked in.

Andy had his back to her so he didn't see her, but she saw him and stopped dead in her tracks.

What the heck is he doing here and when did he get back? It was suddenly like they were the only two in the room, he knew she was in the room, he could feel her presence. He turned around and looked straight into her eyes. He thought she looked great in her mint green dress; he couldn't take his eyes off her as she started across the room towards him. It was like everyone knew something was going to happen, so they all left the room.

She walked up to him and said, "Well look what the cat dragged in . You think you can leave without telling anyone where you have gone and just waltz right back into everyone's life."

Oh yeah she is mad, he thought. "Hello Susan, nice to see you too."

"Don't you nice to see me, what the heck? Do you have any idea how you made me feel? I can't believe I ever let you touch me; you just used me! Well you can leave now I'm over it!"

She turned around intending on leaving the room but Andy reached for her arm, Susan whipped around and growled, "Get your hands off of me."

"Now wait a minute, Susan. I'm sorry you felt like that but it couldn't be helped."

"Yeah right whatever!"

Just then Tony came into the room and asked, "Susan, Are you ok?"

"Yes, Tony I'm fine," she walked out of the room with him leaving Andy standing there staring after her.

Geez he had messed up what in the world he never thought how she would have looked at it. Andy was livid and he just walked right out of the house without saying anything to anyone and went home. Crap! He thought as he drove home, well it looked like she had found herself someone else, anyway. He drove home and went in thinking he would just go to bed; he wanted to forget all about this night, and the gut-wrenching sight of Susan in another man's arms.

The next day was Christmas and Andy had hardly slept at all, he felt awful, and so lonely. He decided he may as well get something productive done; besides he needed the distraction, so he went to his office to work. He threw everything he had into his work in the days, weeks and months ahead; he worked late and went in early. He lost weight and had circles under his eyes; in short he looked like crap.

Susan was shook up too, she didn't know he was back, and why was he here at her family's house. Tony asked her if she was ok and she told him, "I'm fine I just wasn't expecting to see him here."

Tony asked, "Who was he?"

"He was my ex-boyfriend; it was a relationship that had hurt me very much. I don't really want to talk about it right now."

"If you are sure you're ok, then we will drop it. You must know how strong my feelings for you are becoming, so if you have unfinished business with him please tell me."

Susan reassured him, "No Tony, he is my past and I'm in this with you now."

Tony smiled down at her and gave her a sweet gentle kiss. Susan and Tony had a wonderful rest of the night as he set out to help her forget about her earlier upset. She was glad she had brought him home with her for Christmas, he seemed to be having a good time and her parents seemed to like him. Susan did plan asking her mom why Andy was here, at their party, and when did he get back. Why hadn't she told her? Oh her mom was gonna get it when Christmas was over; she was going to have a serious talk with her.

Susan got swept away enjoying the holidays with her family and Tony that before she knew it, the day had come to go back to school. She was in her bedroom packing when her mom came in to say goodbye. Susan finally asked the question that had been plaguing her for days, "Mom there is one thing I have to know. Why was Andy here for our Christmas Eve party, and when did he get back?"

Patty sat on the bed and asked Susan to sit with her, she told her about the phone call he had received in the middle of the night and his rush to get back to the Bahamas to see his grandmother. She told her about his grandmother passing away and how he didn't make it there in time before she passed. She explained that he had to stay there to take care of all of his grandmother's things. She tried her best to help her understand why he had to be gone for so long.

"I see, that's awful, Mom, but it still doesn't make sense. He could have wrote or called, but he chose not to for all these months. I'm sorry mom but he hurt me and that is not excuse enough for me to forgive him. All he had to do was pick up a phone; it would have only taken him 5 minutes to fill me in. He claimed that he loved me, but he walked away and never once tried to contact me through all of this?"

"Yes, Susan, you are right; but he just didn't think about it, he was so distracted and caught up in trying to get back here. I should have told you I invited him."

"It's ok Mom, but please tell me next time."

Patty helped Susan finish her packing and the two women headed downstairs and outside to where Tony was waiting on her. Her dad was there waiting to say goodbye. Susan hugged each of her parents and promised she would be home again soon, her parents told Tony they were happy he had joined them for Christmas and that he was welcome back anytime. Tony and Susan headed back to school, talking about the fun times they had over break; he told her he liked her parents and she let him know how happy that made her.

They arrived back at school tired and ready to unwind. Tony took his stuff and headed off; he told Susan he would call her tomorrow. Christmas break was over and the girls fell back into their routine with classes, work, and dating when time permitted.

Chapter Twenty

Four years later.

ANDY HAD MADE it big, finding great success with his business. Since moving back he had expanded offices all over. He threw all of his time into his work after he had seen Susan on that Christmas Eve. It had been a long time but he had finally got over her enough that he was dating again, but nothing serious. He didn't plan on giving his heart to anyone else, ever again, he just wanted to have a good time with the women he dated and let that be it. He figured since Susan thought he was a love 'em and leave 'em type, he might as well live up to it. He was proud of himself, he had made it big in his business and he was now a millionaire that could afford anything he wanted, but as far as his personal life, he was lonely.

There was nothing like having a social life where he could have a different lady on his arm every night if he wanted too. He had tried dating plenty of these ladies, but none of them measured up to Susan. None of them had captured his heart just the way that she had. How he wished he could go back to that night, he would have left her a note or called… something, anything to save their relationship. It was his fault, he knew he had hurt her and he didn't blame her for feeling the way she did, but dang it, did she have to be so stubborn. Andy didn't have time to think about all of these 'what ifs,' he had so much going on in his business. He had just found out that one of his most valuable employees in marketing was quitting. He was very great at his job and had been with his company ever since he had opened up his office here in Florida, he hated to lose him. Jeff knew the marketing world inside and out. He had contacts everywhere including lot of people that Andy didn't know. Andy hated that he was leaving, but he understood, he had recently gotten married and the couple was moving to be closer to his wife's family. Andy told him he always had a job if ever he wanted to come back, now he had to get busy trying to find someone to fill his shoes. Jeff told him if he wanted to hire an apprentice right out of school, he would be happy to stay and train them so they would know how he did everything. Andy told him that he would appreciate his assistance in preparing his replacement and Jeff agreed to stay until someone was hired, and trained to replace him.

Meanwhile, Susan, Carol and Vickie had all graduated a few months earlier. Carol left Susan and Vickie back in Florida as she traveled to New York where she was hired as a nurse. Carol wrote them and told them about the job she had gotten in a pediatrician's office. Susan and Vickie were very proud of her, but they missed her. Vickie and Susan stayed in their apartment and found work locally after graduating. Vickie found a job with a contractor, doing all the interior design on the new houses. Susan signed on as a marketing assistant with a global company, learning all the ropes of the business. Susan eventually took over as the marketing director when the one who was training her left.

Susan had learned a lot from the previous director and was doing really well in her position. Vickie came home in tears one night and Susan asked her what was wrong?

"Oh Susan they are done with all the houses that I was contracted for so now I'm out of work until I find something else."

Susan hugged her and reassuringly, "Vickie, don't worry, something will turn up. You are brilliant, and so talented that any company would be lucky to have you on their team."

The next day while Susan went to work, Vickie was out looking for a new job when her cell phone rang, it was Carol, "Hi Girl, how are you doing?"

"Good," Vickie filled Carol in on what had happen and that she was out looking for a new job.

"I am so sorry to hear that but I know you will find something soon."

They friends talked for a while, catching up on each other's lives when Carol said. "Well, my break is over and I have to get back to work. Love ya girl, y'all stay in touch. I miss y'all! Please tell Susan Hi and that I love her too."

"Ok I will," as Vickie hung up, her phone rang again, this time it was Susan.

She was sobbing into the phone so Vickie asked, "What's wrong Susan?"

Susan told her she needed to go home, her mom had called and her dad was in an accident and was in the hospital. Susan asked Vickie, "Can you meet me at the apartment in 20 minutes?"

"Sure, I'll see ya there."

When Vickie arrived back at their apartment Susan was packing, throwing everything she would need onto her bed. "Vickie, I've been thinking, since you are out of work, why don't you and I move back home? From what my mom said it looks lik I'm going to have to be there for awhile to help her out with my dad and my brother. Besides, I kinda miss home. What do you think?"

Vickie thought about Susan's idea for a few minutes before replying, "You're right Susan, I miss it too. What better time to move back than when I'm out of work. What about your job?"

"I took a leave of absences for now because of the accident but when I find something there I will just explain to them that my mom needs my help and I'll agree to come back long enough to work out my two week notice if they want me to."

"Okay, so what do we do with all of our stuff here?"

"Well," Susan replied, "Maybe we can find a place back home and live together, in which case we can keep it all. I will be closer to home and if mom needs me to stay at the hospital at night and help her out that way, it won't be that bad what do you think?"

Vickie had started gathering up her own clothes and necessities as well, "I say we go home now and then see what we can find. Once we find a place, we can get some help to bring our furniture back what do you think?"

"Sounds like a plan, now go finish your packing. I need to hurry, mom didn't tell me everything and I'm really worried about my dad."

Thirty minutes later the girls were on their way home. They made record time and Susan dropped Vickie off at her parent's house, "I will call you as soon as I know what is going on."

"Okay, I'll start looking for work tomorrow and see if there are any apartments available in town," Vickie knew her parents would be happy to have her home even if she did move in with Susan. An apartment in town would still be a lot closer than their old apartment.

"Okay, I'll talk to you soon," Susan turned her car around and headed towards the hospital. She arrived and found her dad's room; her mom was there waiting for her, she met her out in the hall.

"Susan I'm so glad you're here, he's in really bad shape."

"What happened Mom?"

"He has been in a car accident and he is in ICU in a coma right now. They don't know if he will make it."

Susan cried, hugging her mom, "I should have been here."

"Hush now, you dad loves you and wanted you to get a good education." Susan knew he loved her and she tried to be brave, but she was so scared.

"Where is Teddy at Mom, he should be here with you."

"Oh he's here, I just talked him into going to the cafeteria to get something to eat before you arrived."

Susan and her mom sat there until their visiting time was over. Since her dad was in the ICU, they were only allowed into his room for 10 minutes every four hours. They went to ICU waiting room and Susan asked her mom, "When did the accident happen?"

"Last night, in the middle of the night, I waited until this morning to call you because I didn't even know myself. Someone found the wreck on the road at six o'clock this morning and called 911. As soon as I found out I rushed over here and then I called you as soon as I finished the paper work. Susan, I'm a nervous wreck. I've spent all of my life with him and I don't want to lose him," Patty sobbed.

Susan hugged her mom to her and tried to reassure her, "I know Mom, its ok he's gonna make it you'll see," hoping she was right.

Just then her brother came into the waiting room. Seeing Susan there he ran over to her and took her into his arms, he was so glad to see her.

Susan hugged her brother tight and told him, "Hey Teddy, it's gonna be ok."

"I know, but I sure am glad you're here."

Later on that day, Susan called Vickie and filled her in on what had happened. Vickie told her, "I'm so sorry, I'll be praying for him and I am here if you need me."

"Thank you. I'll give you a call back in a few days unless anything changes. I'm planning to stay at the hospital for as long as my mom needs me here"

That night Susan talked to the doctors and they told here, "It is just a waiting game now to see if he will wake up. He has had surgery and we have done everything we can to save him. Now it's up to him, his body needs time to heal."

Susan talked her mom into going home to get some sleep and told her she would stay tonight. She told her mom that she needed to rest and stay strong for daddy when he woke up because he would really need her then. Reluctantly, her mom agreed and took Teddy home with her. Before long, word of the accident had spread throughout their small town and the next day people started showing up at their home and the hospital with all kinds of food. It was so nice of everyone; a lot of them didn't know Susan had gotten back into town so they were surprised and excited to see her, even though she knew that she looked like crap. She had slept in the chair in the waiting room last night, what little sleep she got. It was now 3 o'clock pm the next day and she still hadn't gone home to shower, change or anything else. She just couldn't bring herself to leave, her mom fussed and did all she could to get Susan to take a break, but Susan wouldn't budge. Vickie came by the hospital around four and brought Susan a pair of clean sweat pants and a t-shirt, they were baggy on her but she didn't care, they were comfortable. She washed off as best as she could in the hospital restroom and changed into the clean clothes. Susan thanked Vickie and gave her a hug. Vickie told her it was no problem and pleaded with her to get some rest.

"I called Carol and told her what happened, she wanted me to tell you how sorry she is and that she would be praying for him."

Susan gave her hug and cried. Vickie asked, "Do you want or need me to do anything else?"

"No it's ok, I'll be fine."

"Okay, if you're sure. I'm going to look for a job again tomorrow and also an apartment for us if that's okay with you?"

"Yes, that's fine."

Vickie told Susan goodbye and headed out of the hospital. A couple of hours later Susan sat alone on the couch in the waiting room while her mom and brother left to get something to eat. She was half asleep when she heard someone come up beside her and she felt the couch dip when they sat down. She just assumed it was a visitor for one of the other patients and dozed back off. Andy had heard about Susan's dad and came by to see if the family needed anything, he didn't think about Susan being there. As he walked down the hall at the hospital he saw Susan on the couch alone, he didn't know where her mom was and didn't see anyone else around either. She looked worn out, her big baggy clothes made her look so little and lost that he just wanted to sit down and hold her. As he approached her on the sofa, he realized she was asleep and probably needed the rest if the dark circles under her eyes were any indication. Even in her disheveled state, she was still beautiful to him.

Andy sat down beside her and she barely stirred, he reached over and pulled her head down onto his lap so she could stretch out in her sleep. He didn't know how long he sat there holding her, but it still felt good and right. Susan felt something hard, yet kind of soft, under her head and there was an arm on her waist. What in the world she thought as she came awake. She opened her eyes and was shocked to see who was sitting there holding her while she slept. Rage ran through her, if he thought he could just sit down by her and hold her like that he had another thing coming. When did he even get here? She sat up quickly and scooted to the other end of the couch.

Susan gave him a look and asked, "What you are doing here?"

He sat there smiling like an idiot, "I came by to see how your dad was and it looked like you were going to get a crick in your neck so I sat here and let you use me as a pillow. Besides, I didn't see your mom anywhere and I wanted to find out if there was any change with him."

"Well you could have asked a nurse!"

"You know they won't tell me anything since I'm not family, and I was concerned about you. You looked so lost and tired; I wanted to see if you needed anything or if I could do anything for you."

"It's a little late to be so concerned for me don't you think. I mean, where was all this concern when you left? Oh never mind! I'm tired. What do you want?"

"I told you," he said, "how is your dad?"

"There is no change," Susan said, "Now please leave."

"Okay, but if you need anything, please call me."

"Don't count on it."

Andy got up and started down the hall toward the exit when he saw Patty. Susan's mom smiled and said, "Andy, how nice of you to stop by."

"I wanted to check and see if I could do anything for y'all."

"Thank you, that was nice of you, but right now we are fine."

"Okay, well, if anything changes, or if you need anything, please call me. Goodbye."

Susan sat on the couch watching the exchange between them. Patty walked over to the couch and said "That was nice of him, wasn't it?"

"Yeah right," Susan said. Patty let it drop, she didn't want to get into it so she told Susan to go home for a while and take her brother so they could get some rest. She would stay tonight since Susan had stayed last night. "Are you sure mom? I've been asleep, I can stay."

"No, you go rest and get cleaned up. You can come back tomorrow. I promise to call you if there is any change."

Susan leaned over and kissed her mom goodbye and said, "Come on Teddy, let's go home.

Several weeks after the accident, Susan's dad came out of the coma and before long he was being released to go home. Susan was so excited, they all were. The family understood how lucky they were to have Derek back with them but knew that he still had a tough road ahead of him. He would need regular physical therapy and there would still be pain as his injuries healed. The family was willing to do whatever it took to help him heal. As they were preparing for Derek to go home, Susan told her parents she and Vickie were moving back. They were so excited to have her back home, but she also told them they planned to get an apartment in town. They were so thrilled that she was going to be close to home that they weren't even disappointed that she wouldn't be moving back into her old bedroom.

Life could finally start getting back to normal. Vickie called and told her she had found a job and they had a few appointments today to look at apartments. After looking at the apartments that Vickie had set up, they knew that they would need to continue their search. They met at the café to lay out their plan and, as promised, Nancy gave them free chocolate pie. They looked through the paper and found a few more places to check out. Nancy told them she was so glad they were back and now that they were finished with school, they could afford their own chocolate pie. The girls laughed and told her she was okay with that. After enjoying the pie, they set out to check on the places they had found in the paper. The first one was a NO. It had bugs everywhere. The next few wouldn't work for them either, one was too small and one was really nice but they couldn't afford it. They were just about to give up but they had one more on their list to look at. As they drove to the last place they recalled their first apartment hunt and they realized that it could take them a while to find something that would suit them.

They pulled into the driveway of their final prospect for today and they were instantly impressed. The realtor met them at the door with the keys. As they walked through the house, both girls fell in love with it. It wasn't a big house, but it had a nice sized living room, a small kitchen and a small dining room with a patio door out onto a small deck which they both liked. There were two bedrooms one had a bath but the other bath was in the hall. The second bedroom was a good size so they didn't mind that it didn't have a built in bathroom. Now the big question was how much? The realtor told them it was a steal, in this nice neighborhood, and within walking distance of the beach all for only $750.00 a month. The girls stepped out onto the deck to talk it over.

"I have already found work and now that you can look for a job, it won't take you long, so what do you think?", Vickie asked Susan.

Susan told her, "I have some saved up; it should help us until I get a job."

"Sooo? Is that a yes? Have we found our new place?"

"Well, we both love it, it's right here in town and close to the beach, we know that we can afford it, of course it's a YES!"

They went back inside to tell the realtor that they were going to take the house. They signed the lease and paid the deposit and the first month's rent and the realtor left them with the keys.

The girls spun around in circles taking in their new home as they were overcome with laughter. They were home, it was real, they were moving back to their hometown and they had found a house that was perfect for them. Nothing could be more perfect than this moment.

Susan looked over at Vickie and asked, "Did we just move back home? Did we really just sign a lease on this house???"

"YES! Now which room do you want?", Vickie laughed.

Susan told her, "you take the one with the bathroom; I can use the one in the hallway I don't mind."

"Okay, if you're sure, I'm not going to turn down the master bedroom." They walked through the house again; the living room had beige carpet so all of their stuff from the other apartment would fit in there ok. Susan's bedroom had light blue carpet which happened to be her favorite color, while Vickie's bedroom had a rose colored carpet. The kitchen and dining room both had hardwood floors which they loved. Their new house was perfect, now they had to see who they could get to help them move their stuff back.

Vickie said "I've already talked to my dad and he said he could help us with his truck and with my car and your car we can load everything up. We'll just need someone strong for the heavy things."

Susan offered to call Tony and see if he could help. Susan and Tony had broken up a few years ago because they realized that they were better off as friends. They kept in touch and he had become one of her best friends. Vickie told her to go ahead and call so they could set it all up. She called Tony and caught him up on the latest news on her father and then told him that she and Vickie had found a house back home and asked if he would be willing to help them load up their old apartment. He told her he was available whenever she needed him and that he was excited for her. He told her that he had been praying for her father and hoped that he continued to improve and asked her to give her parents his love. Before he would let her off the phone, he asked about Andy. He asked if she had seen him again, if they had talked and if anything had changed. Susan filled him in on the episode at the hospital but told him that was it, she hadn't seen him again and she would be perfectly fine if she never saw him again. Tony asked her if she was sure that she was truly done with Andy, this was a discussion they had many times over the years and Susan told him that nothing had changed. She told Tony that she would see him soon and thanked him for agreeing to help her move.

Finally with all that settled Susan headed back into the house to let Vickie know they had the muscle they needed to move. She said, "Now I have to get busy and find a job."

"Good luck it only took me a few days so maybe it will be just as easy for you."

The girls decided to go back to the café and get supper to celebrate their new home. It had gotten late and they hadn't even realized it. Once back at the café they ordered burgers and fries with milkshakes to celebrate. They had had a great day, now all they had to do was get Susan a job.

Susan said, "I will start my job search tomorrow morning I will get the paper and check out the help wanted ads." After supper, Vickie told her she would call her after she checked with her dad to find out when he was free to help them move.

Susan said, "Okay, I will call my job there and see if they want me to come back for a two weeks' notice or how they want to handle that."

With a tentative plan established, the girls headed home to their parents' houses. When Susan got home, she told her mom about the house that she and Vickie had found. Her mom was thrilled to learn that it wasn't very far away. She and her mom then went over what all they needed to do to help her dad recover; he had to take physical therapy which wouldn't be a problem because she could take him to that while Teddy was at school, but there were a few things that they needed to do to make the house more comfortable for her dad that she could help with.

Patty told Susan to go ahead and look for work and get moved into the new house and then she could come over and help her in the evenings if she wasn't too tired. Susan asked, "Are you sure mom, I don't mind helping."

"Yes I'm sure, you have to get yourself situated now and if I need you more I will let you know."

Susan smiled, "Okay, I love you mom!"

Chapter Twenty-One

On Saturday Vickie, Susan and Susan's parent's made the trip to pack up and move them from their old apartment. It took them the entire afternoon and evening to pack up all of their belongings and load the vehicles. Vickie and Susan had left in such a hurry when Susan's father was in his accident, they hadn't even discussed moving before that trip, so none of their belongings were packed up. Tony was a tremendous help to them all, who knew that he could pack so efficiently. He even volunteered a few friends to help with the loading so they had some extra strong bodies to help out. When the apartment was empty, Susan decided to take one last walk-through. She wanted to have one last look at the place where she had developed her independence, she was locking in memories that she would keep forever. As she stood in the living room she thought back to that first night the girls had spent in the house, she recalled the feast they had enjoyed and the sense of excitement that was burning within them. She was startled from her reverie by the feel of arms coming around her waist, but she knew instantly that Tony had come up behind her; she had not forgotten the feeling of his body against hers or the smell of his body wash.

"You know right here is where we shared our first kiss, on your sofa over Thanksgiving break. I thought you were an unattainable dream until you invited me back here at the pizza shop that night," Tony whispered in her ear.

"Oh, Tony, I'm so sorry, where did we go wrong?" Susan sighed.

"I think we both know the answer to that, but I have often wondered what would have happened if I had met you six months earlier, if your heart didn't already belong to someone else," he held her a little tighter as he shared the thoughts he'd kept to himself for so long.

"Tony, I told you, Andy does not have my heart anymore. We are over, have been over for years. I know you don't believe me, but I feel nothing but hatred for that man! He took my love and threw it away, he doesn't deserve me and he never will. I hate to think that his ghost might have cost me the best guy I have ever known," she cried in indignation.

"Sweetie, there is a very thin line between love and hate, and anyone who knows you can see the pain written on your face anytime he is near or even when his name is mentioned. Have you even tried to talk to him since that party at your parents? Maybe you should give him a chance to explain things. I don't blame you at all for our break up, and you will never lose me! You are and will always be one of my best friends. Your family gave me my first real Christmas and I will treasure those memories for as long as I live," he lifted her eyes to his, "Now I want you to make me a promise."

"Anything, Tony, as long as it's within my means, I would do anything for you. You weren't the only one that gained something from our time together. You taught me that I had value and restored my faith in men, you showed me love even when I didn't deserve it, and you have been my rock for four years. If it was in my reach I'd give you the stars, so what would you like from me?"

"My promise isn't going to be as easy as grabbing a few stars, I hate to tell you. But if you keep it, I promise that you will thank me someday."

"Okay Tony, out with it, you are starting to scare me," Susan laughed nervously.

"Here it is; if and when you see Andy again, give him a chance to explain what happened all those years ago. I am not asking you to trust him, or forget the pain he caused you, but I am asking that you just listen. He loved you, and he probably still does, because from what I have seen, that kind of love is the lifetime kind. I never told you this, but when I took that walk on the beach to give you some family time before we came home from that first Christmas break, I ran into Andy on the beach. He was devastated, I could see it in his eyes, and we talked. I asked him how he could just throw you aside like he did and we had a very long talk, I won't tell you everything he said, because those are things he needs to tell you himself, but I will tell you I made him a promise that day. He made me promise him that I would never hurt you, that I would hold onto you and make sure that you knew every day that you were special to me, and he made me promise that if you ever needed anything at all, I would call him. He loved you so much that he didn't fight for you, but he let you go so that you could have a chance at happiness. My only regret, is that no matter how much I wanted it to be so, I never loved you quite that much. You mean the world to me, and you are one of my dearest friends, but I could never love you quite as much as he did. So, if you are serious about keeping your promise to me, give him a chance to explain and then you can decide whether to walk away or give him another chance. But if it turns out how I suspect it will, I expect an invitation to your wedding!"

Chapter Twenty-Two

THE NEXT MORNING Susan woke up early to eat a good breakfast and get ready for her interview. Looking through her closet, she decided she needed a new outfit for her interview; she wanted to make a great first impression because she really needed this job. It was only eight in the morning and her interview wasn't until two o'clock so she had plenty of time to go shopping. Susan took a quick trip to the mall and found exactly what she wanted; just trying on the new suit had filled her with confidence. After a long hot shower to help her relax, she slipped into her new suit. The powder blue suit was paired with a silver sleeveless shell under her jacket that gave it just a little bit of character and shine. She dressed it up with silver heels, a simple silver chain and silver hoop ear rings. Surveying herself in the mirror she was very happy with what she saw. I would definitely hire me, she thought. Susan grabbed her necessities out of her purse and slipped them into her new little silver clutch purse, she was ready to go. She checked herself one last time and headed out the door.

Susan was nervous when she headed out for her interview; she had learned from the ad the position was to replace someone who was leaving the company. If she got the job, he would stay on for a few weeks to train her and help her acclimate to the job and the clients. She wished she had taken time to learn more about the company that she was interviewing with so she would be better prepared for her interview. She found the building without any problem since she had lived here her whole life. The company was housed in an old warehouse building that had been remodeled into offices. Susan parked her car went inside where she met the receptionist.

"Hello, I'm Susan Lewis and I'm here for an interview."

"Hello Miss Lewis, I'm Sharon, if you will please take a seat I will call HR and tell them you are here."

"Thank you," Susan turned to find a seat in the waiting area.

A few minutes later, a gentleman approached her in the waiting room, "Miss Lewis," he asked?

Standing she nodded, "Yes, I'm Susan Lewis."

"Hello, I'm Jeff. If you will follow me, I will take you to the conference room where we will be conducting your interview today." Together they walked to the conference room, "Have a seat please, and we will get started momentarily."

Susan sat in the chair that Jeff had indicated and made small talk with him for a few minutes while they waited for the head of HR to arrive. "Hello Miss Lewis, I'm Beth, head of HR. I've asked Jeff to join us today, because if you are hired, it will be his vacancy you will be filling and he will be training you, to make sure you know all about our clients and so on before he leaves us for good."

The interview lasted about two hours before they told Susan that she was hired. Susan was so excited; it was all she could do to stay in her seat while they went over the paperwork she needed to complete for personnel. Once her paperwork was complete, they welcomed her to the company and told her that the owner was away at other offices. She wouldn't meet him till he was back in town in a month or two.

Susan questioned, "Doesn't he have to approve my being hired?"

Jeff reassured her, "Don't worry if I approve of you he will too, just do your job and he will be fine with you."

During the interview, Beth had asked when she was able to start work; she told them that she could be available on Monday of next week. When her interview was over, Jeff and Beth walked her back to the lobby and told her that they would see her on Monday. Leaving the interview, Susan headed to her parents' house so she could tell her mom the good news. On her way to see her mom, she called Carol to tell her all about her new job. Her mother was thrilled to hear that she had found work and she made plans to cook her a celebratory dinner later on that week. When Susan got home she called her former employer to let them know she had found another job, she explained that she had decided to move back home to help her mother care for her father as he recovered and so she would be unable to return to work. She offered to work out her two weeks' notice if they really needed her to. She felt guilty for leaving them in a lurch but they reassured her that they understood and released her from having to work through the two weeks. They told her that if anything ever changed and she needed a job, she was welcome to come back since they hated to lose her.

When Vickie got home had supper was done and Susan was waiting for her on the couch with a huge smile on her face. She came in and asked, "Okay, what's up? I have waited all day to hear about your interview and I need to know what happened."

Susan stood slowly and then yelled "I got the job!!!" Susan was so excited that she was talking a mile a minute as she filled Vickie in.

"This is great news! I am so happy for you!" Vickie congratulated her.

"Yes, our lives are finally coming together," Susan exclaimed!

Vickie was surprised that Susan had cooked supper, she had offered to take her out to celebrate but Susan told her that supper was ready and waiting for her. The girls had and informal supper eating on the couch while they watched TV. Susan filled Vickie in on all the details for her new job, letting her know that she wouldn't start until next week. She wanted time to help her mom make the adjustments for her dad as well as getting settled into their new home.

"Oh yea, I nearly forgot! Mom invited us over for dinner later this week. She wants to celebrate my new job with Dad and Teddy, and you know my mom…she will most likely cook a feast suitable for a small army," Susan said, only half joking.

Vickie laughed, "It is so good to be back in our home town, everything is coming together for us."

It had been two weeks since Susan started her new job and she loved it. Jeff had been impressed with her skills and experience; he assured her she would do really well there as she was already a perfect fit. Susan was making his job easy, with her existing skills; all he had to do was teach her their clients' likes and needs so that she would be able to take over for him. He said he didn't have any worries about her taking over his job as she had proven that she was more than capable to him. On Jeff's last day of work, she asked him if she would ever meet her new boss, he told that when he got back into town he would call a staff meeting to get caught up and she would meet him then. Susan was still nervous about meeting her mysteriously absent boss, but she had heard everyone in the office speaking of him. Everyone told her that he was a fair man who took very good care of his employees.

Susan hoped that the owner would be happy with her work because she enjoyed her new job and her coworkers. She knew she would be happy working here for many years to come. Susan had settled into a routine going to work, and then going by to help her mom if she needed it before heading home. Her dad was doing much better and she figured it wouldn't be long before he would be back to his old self. As much as she loved spending so much time with her parents, she looked forward to a time when her father was able to regain his independence and she would be able to rest. She was also looking forward to having some free time to spend with her friends.

Susan had become fast friends with Jan, one of her coworkers. The ladies often had lunch together and discussed their lives as well as exchanging office gossip. One day, Jan asked if she had met the owner of the company yet? Susan replied, "No, they say he has been out of town since before I got hired."

"Oh!" Jan said, "Well you just wait until you see him, you will know him right off he is a hottie and all the girls in the office drool over him!!"

Susan laughed and said "Oh no, what's his name? I never realized until now that I don't even know my bosses name!"

Jan giggled, "His name is Mr. Boyd, and I can't believe nobody has told you about him yet! Girl he is a hunk. If I had to guess I'd say he is a little older than you and a bachelor."

Susan sighed, "Oh my, he sounds great, but I work for him so I'm not interested in him as anything other than my boss."

Jan giggled, "Girl you just wait until you see him, and you might change your mind about that."

"Okay, okay…I admit you have me wondering what he is really like. Do you know when he will be back?"

Jan pouted, "No, we never know when he's coming or going. He has quite a few companies and he has to travel a lot to check on them. He has made a lot of money in such a short amount of time; they say he is one of the youngest millionaire's in the United States."

"Wow! He must be pretty smart be so rich at such a young age."

"Yeah he's a business genius or so they say. It's lunch time, wanna get outta here for an hour?"

"Sure" Susan said and they walked down the street a few blocks to the café lunch continuing their discussion.

Later that afternoon Jan told Susan, "You be sure wear something nice Monday."

Susan said "Why? What's up?"

"The rumor is, Mr. Boyd might be back in town and, if so he'll be holding a staff meeting and you will definitely want to look your best for him. You know how important first impressions are after all."

Susan laughed, shaking her head at Jan's outright attempt at matchmaking, "Okay, will do." She had to admit she loved her new job and she really wanted to make a great first impression on her new boss. She had already been given more responsibility with Jeff's recommendation. She had been told that once she was able to prove herself she would have even more responsibility someday and eventually she would take over Jeff's old job. She was looking forward to seeing what the future held for her with this company.

Chapter Twenty-Three

After work Susan went to see her mom and dad on her way home, she was surprised to see that her dad was in the living room. "Hi dad!"

"Well hun, come on in here and have a seat. You've been working a lot lately, so how do you like your new job? Are you all settled in at your new place here in town," he had so many questions and was excited to actually be awake when she came by today. He was usually napping when she came by and he had missed her. Susan smiled and told her dad all about her job and the house she was renting with Vickie.

He told her, "I'm sure glad you are back in town, you were gone far too long."

"I'm glad to be back too Dad, and I'm sure glad to see you are feeling better."

"Yeah, me too, maybe before too long I can get back to doing a few things around here."

Her mom stepped into the room, "Hi Susan, I've almost got supper done, you can stay and eat with us and I'll send some leftovers home for you and Vickie for the weekend."

Susan laughed, "Okay mom. Between you and Vickie's mom we don't have to cook very often. Y'all always send us food."

Patty explained, "Well we have to cook anyways, and y'all are always working these days. Besides we're both so glad y'all moved back and we want to help you out as much as we can."

Susan laughed, "Well we sure do appreciate it, you two are saving us a fortune on our grocery bill."

After a nice family supper, Susan headed home loaded down with a weekend's worth of leftovers. Just as she was unlocking the front door, Vickie pulled in behind her in the driveway. Watching Vickie walk into the kitchen, Susan laughed, "Looks like your mom and mine had the same idea," as Vickie unloaded dishes onto the kitchen counter.

Vickie laughed incredulously, "You mean you brought leftovers home too?"

"Yeah, maybe we should freeze some of this so we can have it throughout the week."

Vickie agreed, "Way ahead of you, I stopped and bought containers on my way home so we could transfer some of it into single portions and freeze them."

"Cool" said Susan as she pulled all the leftovers back out that she has just put in the refrigerator. They laid all of it out on the counter and then decided what to freeze and what they would have tomorrow. By the time they were done re-packaging all of their leftovers they were onto their mothers' plan. They laughed realizing their moms were trying, in their own way, to say if you live here it won't cost y'all too much. With tonight's leftovers they would have enough food to last them until Wednesday. They had kept out the leftovers that they would want for the weekend the desserts. The leftovers could possibly last them even longer if they decided to cook some nights. It would be nice to just be able to pull out the leftovers if they didn't feel well or if they had worked late. As they discussed the leftovers they suddenly busted out laughing, "Can't you just see us trying to do anything if one of us got sick?"

Susan said "yeah they would both be here in a flash with medicine and food." They both laughed all the way into the living room. As they settled down on the couch to watch some TV, Susan told Vickie about that she might finally be meeting her boss on Monday.

"Wow!" Vickie said, "I bet you can't wait after all the stuff you've heard about him. You'd better wear one of your sexiest work outfits."

Susan laughed, "Yeah right, like I would even get a look from him in that way. He's rich and he's used to all those uppity super model looking women so he won't even notice me. That's fine by me though, I just want to work for him.

"Yeah, but, a little fringe benefits would be nice too."

Susan blushed, "No, it wouldn't hurt, but oh well he may not even be as good looking as they say."

After the movie Susan said, "I'm heading to bed, I'm beat. Whatcha going to do tomorrow?"

Vickie said, "Oh I don't know…I'm thinking about going to the beach you want to go?"

"Sure, but let's sleep late and I'll pack us a picnic."

"Ok," said Vickie, "then when we are done on the beach we can go to a few of those shops down there."

"Sounds like a plan! See ya in the morning."

The next day the girls slept in till around ten, Susan packed them a picnic lunch and they headed to the beach. They rented one of the beach umbrellas so they wouldn't get too much sun and laid out there towels. Vickie pulled out a small radio and turned it on so they could listen to music while eating their lunch and laying out. The girls were having a great day, the sun was shining and the guys on the beach were so hot. They laid out watching them play volleyball; enjoying the show as their muscles flexed and moved and their chests began to glisten from sweat as the game went on. They giggled when one of the hunks came over to get the ball as it rolled over beside them. Susan told Vickie, "You go girl! That guy is totally checking you out."

Vickie blushed, "Oh Susan, stop it! He was not; he just came over to get their ball."

"If that's what you think…" Susan teased.

After a few more minutes of watching the game, they went back in the water to cool off. When they were good and wet, they came back to their pallet and lay down. They helped each other put sunscreen on and prepared to work on their tans. They lay there tanning until the sun started to set and the air grew cool. Susan and Vickie put on their cover-ups, packed up their cooler and towels and loaded them in the car. Ready to do some shopping, they walked around to some of the shops to browse. After going through about twenty shops, they decided to head home. They had both spent a little too much money and were tired from their long day in the sun.

Arriving back at their house, they unloaded the car and headed for the showers. They were definitely grateful for the leftovers today as they popped their plates in the microwave to heat up before collapsing on their couch to watch a movie while they ate. While they were eating they looked at each other and started laughing. Susan said, "Oops, looks like we got a little too much sun today. We look like lobsters."

Vickie laughed, "I guess we stayed out a little too long. We'll have to make sure we put on some aloe before we go to bed, we can't have you looking like a lobster when you meet the boss man on Monday!"

Chapter Twenty-Four

BY THE TIME Monday morning came around, Susan had a healthy glow to her skin the red from her burn had turned into a nice tan. Looking through her closet, she chose to wear one of her new outfits to work. She told herself that she picked it out, not because she may or may not meet the boss today, but because she had some color now and it looked good on her, or at least that's what she was telling herself.

When she got to work, everyone seemed to be in a panic; finding Jan she asked her what was going on?

"He's here! Well not yet, but the word is, he is in town and will probably be in later on today. Everyone is trying to get things in order for the staff meeting, because he will want one if he comes in. Susan sat at her desk and told Jan if she needed her to help with anything to just let her know.

Jan warned her, "You might want to get everything together that you have worked on since you started here, he will want to meet you and see the progress you have made."

"Oh," Susan said in exasperation, "Well it would have been nice if you had told me this Friday."

"I'm sorry, but if I had told you sooner, you would have fussed and worried all weekend for nothing. You are doing a great job."

"Thanks," Susan said, "but I would still like to have had some time to prepare."

"Uh huh, looks like you are already prepared. Is that a new dress," Jan asked?

Susan smiled, "Well it can't hurt to look my best," then winked at her.

The morning passed quickly when Jan came to get Susan, "Let's go to lunch before your meeting with Mr. Boyd at 1 o'clock."

"What?" Susan asked, "So he is here?"

"Yes," Jan told her, "He's up in his office. Now come on I'm hungry."

Andy had gotten back into town the night before and he was so happy to be home, he was looking forward to getting back into the swing of things at his main office. He talked to Jeff several times and knew they had hired his replacement. Jeff was confident enough in her abilities; she was doing everything right so he left a few weeks ago. He wasn't as sure about it so he set up a meeting to go over her work and see how she was doing. He couldn't believe his luck, or that she was really working for him. He had no doubt that she didn't know he was the owner of this company and her boss, or she would never have agreed to work there. He couldn't believe she had moved home and he wondered if she was still dating that guy. He had been so hurt when he saw her at the Christmas party and he couldn't believe she wouldn't even listen or talk to him. When he went to the hospital, to check on her father, she had been quite upset with him as well, and all he wanted to do was help.

If that was how she wanted it, so be it. He thought he had gotten over her, but now with her working for him, could he handle that? He couldn't wait to see the look on her face when she walked in for their meeting and saw who her boss was. No doubt, she would receive the shock of her life and she would not like it. Laughing at the images in his mind, he sat down behind his desk to wait for the meeting. He called his secretary to call her office and tell her exactly what files to bring to their meeting.

Susan's phone rang just as she got back from lunch; Mr. Boyd's secretary was on the line, calling to tell her what files he would like her to bring to the meeting. She told Susan he didn't see any point in her bringing everything, just those would do.

"Thank you," Susan said.

"You're welcome," she said, "See you in a bit." Susan gathered up the requested files and went into the rest room to touch up her make-up check her dress before heading to his office.

Andy stood with his back to the door, looking out the window. He was just wondering what was keeping her when there was a timid knock on his door. He called, "Come in." Susan had shut the door and was turning back around just as he turned back from the window.

"Hello Susan."

Susan couldn't believe her eyes, "Andy," she whispered, "What are you doing here? I'm sorry I must have gotten the room wrong, but why are you here?"

Andy smiled, "You look beautiful Susan," he said as he took her by the arm and led her to a seat. "Here, have a seat, I think I have some explaining to do."

Susan couldn't believe it, what the crap is he doing here? "I don't have time for this," she told him as she started to rise.

"Sit down Susan; do you not remember my last name?"

She looked at him in confusion, "Uh no, why would I? I've spent the last four years trying to forget you."

Andy chuckled, coughing to cover up laughter, "Well, Susan, let me introduce myself," holding out his hand to shake hers he said, "I'm Mr. Boyd, Mr. Andy Boyd, your boss, I believe."

Susan looked at him in shock, her face flushed, "Oh No! I mean what the… I can't work for you. I didn't, I mean, no one ever said your first name. Wait a minute; you're the millionaire they all talk about?"

Andy laughed, "Yeah, I guess I am. Oh come on Susan, sit down and let's talk please. Let me see what you have done? Jeff told me how talented you are and how great your work is, so can you show me your files?" She hugged the files tightly to her chest and he said, "We can do this Susan, we're not kids anymore. We can work together, can't we?"

Still feeling overwhelmed she replied shakily, "I don't know, truthfully, I really don't think so."

"Well let me see what you've done, I may not want you working here anyway," he goaded her. He knew that would do the trick. Susan flung the files at him and sat there fuming.

"Well I am sure I can take my skills somewhere else if you don't like my work. It's probably for the best anyway," she retorted bitterly.

Andy looked at her and sighed, "Susan I was teasing you, there was a time when you could tell when I was just messing with you."

Susan just sat there, staring blankly out the window while he looked everything over; seeing him here today brought back her conversation with Tony and her promise to him. As badly as she wanted to walk out the door right now and never look back, she would keep her promise and at least listen to what he had to say after he finished looking over her files.

Finally done, he looked up at her and immediately apologized, "Susan, you are doing great. Your work is amazing and I was wrong. I'm sorry for doubting you and thinking you couldn't do the job." He stood stepping over to her chair, he took her by the hand and pulled her to her feet and stroked her cheek as he looked into her eyes, praying that she could see the truth in his. "I'm very sorry for hurting you before, more than you can ever know. I know we can't get back what we once had, but I hope you will consider staying here and trying to work together. I'd hate to lose you when you are doing such a great job. My employees all love you and I don't think that they will forgive me if you leave now because of me."

He had pulled her into his arms as he spoke and Susan looked up at him to answer, "Thank you, but I'm not sure this is a good idea. I guess we could give it a try, but I won't make you any promises."

Andy hugged her to him, "Okay, I will have to accept that, but I have missed my best friend."

Susan backed away shaking her head in denial, "This is business, nothing else. You're my boss now."

Andy reached for her, already missing the feel of her in his arms, "Now Susan, we were friends a long time before this."

Susan replied, a note of bitterness and long buried pain in her voice, "Yes we were, but you ruined that, remember? I should make one thing clear to you now; I am only staying here now because of Tony. I made him a promise, and I intend to keep it, if it weren't for him I would have walked out that door as soon as I saw you."

Andy felt a stabbing pain in his chest at her words; she was still with that Tony guy. He didn't quite understand what this promise was she was talking about, but he had to get her out of his office before she saw the effect her words were having on him. "I see, well then, you may go back to your office. This meeting is over, but I'm glad you've agreed to stay. If it weren't for you, we would be lost without Jeff."

Susan grabbed her files and headed back to her office as fast as her legs would carry her. Andy had to laugh, watching her almost run to the elevator as he went around the desk to get a drink. He didn't know which one of them needed that meeting to end more. He couldn't help but think of how beautiful she looked. Her mint green dress showed just the right amount of cleavage while maintaining professionalism and it hugged all of her perfect curves. The skirt came to a stop just above her knees, but when she sat with her legs crossed, he really enjoyed the view. She was still the most beautiful woman he had even seen.

Loosening his tie and collar, Andy could tell working with Susan was going to be harder than he had thought. What was he going to do? She knew her job, of that he was certain; she had done an amazing job since Jeff had left. Heck, she had even secured a few of the clients that Jeff could never get. No way was he going to get rid of her; he would just have to learn to control this attraction and impulses where she was concerned. If he couldn't have her in his life, where she was meant to be, he would settle for working with her, at least it was something.

Chapter Twenty-Five

Stepping off the elevator, Susan made a dash for her office where she locked the door and broke down in tears. How could this happen, she thought, she loved this job but there was no way could she stay here when he was her boss, promise or no promise. Oh Dang it! What am I going to do? Pulling herself together, she grabbed her cell phone to call Vickie.

"Hello," Vickie answered, that was all it took and Susan was crying again. "Who is this," Vickie asked.

"It's m-m-m-m-me, Susan."

"Susan," Vickie asked "what's wrong? Oh gosh is it your dad?"

"No," Susan said, "it's my boss."

"What happened? Didn't he like you? Did you get fired? Talk to me! What's wrong? If that's what it is we'll be ok you can get another job."

Susan laughed at Vickie's rapid-fire round of questions. Sniffling she replied, "No he likes me alright, but... my boss is Andy."

"Oh NO!" Vickie cried, "What are you going to do?"

"I don't know," Susan whispered, her voice shaking again, "I just had to call you. I just got out of a meeting with him and that's when I discovered he was my boss and worse he is the millionaire the girls are always talking about."

"Wow!" Vickie said, "That might not be a bad thing if you and he ever get back together."

"Yeah right! That's not ever gonna happen." Susan paused before sighing, "Okay, Vickie, I'm sorry I called you at work. I just needed to talk for a minute. Thank you for listening and letting me dump all this on you."

"It's okay," Vickie said, "We can talk more about this tonight."

"I'll see you tonight Vickie."

"Okay," Vickie said, "And Susan, please don't quit your job just yet. At least, let's talk about it first please."

"Okay," Susan replied before she hung up the phone. Susan did her best to pull herself together so she could finish the rest of her day. Thankfully, Jan was too busy to check on her as she didn't want to talk to anyone right now. She sure wasn't going to tell anyone here about her and Andy's past.

Finally, after what seemed like days, her crazy day had come to an end. She waited until she thought everyone else was gone before emerging from her office to leave the building. After work Susan went straight home, she needed to talk to Vickie and figure out what she was going to do. Vickie wasn't home yet so she fixed herself a nice hot bubble bath and soaked in the water until it grew cool. Feeling better after her soak, she put on some old jogging pants and a tank top then headed to the kitchen to find something for supper. Just as she reached the kitchen, Vickie came in and asked, "What's up Chickie??"

Susan laughed, "Not much, what would you like for supper?"

She and Vickie decided which leftovers to heat up when Vickie said, "Pop it in the microwave and pour the wine, I'll be just a minute."

After a quick shower, Vickie came back down in a pair of shorts and a tank top. Sniffing the air she remarked, "Yum, this smells good!" They took their plates and the wine to the living room where they clicked on the TV while they ate. They joked that the supper table never got used in their house because they always ate on the couch while watching TV.

The next day at work, Susan decided she could handle working with Andy; she would just avoid him at all cost, unless there was a meeting or something, she wouldn't have to see him at all. She decided that she was just going to think of him as the man who signed her paychecks, nothing more, nothing less. She worked the rest of the week without so much as running into him in the hall, which was exactly what she wanted. I can do this; I can handle working here she thought as she got on the elevator to head out for the day. Just as that thought crossed her mind, Andy stepped into the elevator with her. Dang it! It's almost like he knew I was thinking about him or something!

"Hello," Andy said, as he stepped into the elevator. "We have to stop meeting like this, Susan," he joked, flashing her a charming smile."

Ugh! Susan thought, I don't need this. He's too close to me and I don't need to fall for him again. Smiling, she said, "I thought you would be gone by now."

Andy laughed, "Sooo, that's why I haven't seen you all week? You have been trying to avoid me."

Susan hesitated before answering him, "No, that's not it; I was running late leaving and I thought no one else was here."

"Sure," Andy said, "If that's what you want to think. Listen, Susan, lets go out for supper."

"No, thank you." Susan said, "I don't have time, I'm late getting home and I still need to go check on my dad."

"Okay, I'll let you off this time. How is your dad doing, is he better?"

"Yes, thank you," Susan said, "He is doing really well, in fact he is almost as good as new."

The elevator came to a stop and Andy motioned for her to go first, putting his hand on the small of her back to guide her through. She started to say something, but her brain went blank as she felt that familiar tingle suffuse her, it was the one she always felt when he would touch her. Oh! This is not good, she thought, not good at all. Andy told Susan how happy he was to hear that her dad was doing better as he walked her to her car. He told her, "Goodnight," the opened the door for her to get in.

Andy stood there watching her tail lights as she drove off. He thought to himself, That was not a good move touching her like that. He could still feel the heat running up his arm and knew he was in trouble. He had secretly been avoiding her, this week as well, he didn't want to risk something happening between them when she was his employee, not to mention, she had made it perfectly clear to him that there was nothing between them outside of work. He couldn't help wondering if his touch had affected her half as much as it was still affecting him, but that line of thoughts was dangerous.

Oh well, he thought, it was Friday and he decided was going to the bar to drown himself in a couple of beers, he had to get these feelings under control. There was a very important meeting coming up and he needed to be able to work with Susan to keep the account. This was a very important account and he would do whatever it took to keep it, even if he had to work with her every day. It wouldn't be a problem for him, who am I kidding, but could she handle working that closely with him. I guess we will find out next week, he thought. He headed to his car intent on finding someplace to get a beer and relax.

Chapter Twenty-Six

THE WEEKEND WAS over too fast for Susan, she couldn't believe how fast it had flown by. Mondays, ugh, she hated Mondays especially rainy, nasty, dark Mondays. She wished that she could afford to call off and hide from the torrential downpours out there, but she needed the money so she had to get up and go to work; even if she didn't like her boss that much. She had enough concerns with her job right now anyway. She had this one client, he was used to working with Jeff and he had conveniently forgotten to tell her how stubborn and contrary this client was. He sounded like an older man on the phone and he told her wouldn't renew his contract until he talked to the boss, which meant Andy. Ugh! She didn't want to have to go to Andy about this, but what else could she do? She needed this job, even if it meant having to suffer through a meeting with him she would do it.

Susan was sitting in her office getting ready to go to lunch when someone knocked on her door; she figured it was probably Jan wanting to go to lunch together since they usually did, so she called out, "Come in." Andy opened her door and walked in, she couldn't breathe, what the crap does he want now, she thought.

"Hi!" Andy said, "Have you got a minute?"

"Sure." What else could she have said, he owned the place, and he was her boss.

Andy told her, "We have a meeting coming up at two o'clock today with one of our biggest clients. I guess you probably know which one I'm referring to."

Susan laughed and said, "Yeah, that mean old man."

Andy roared with laughter at her all too accurate description, "Yeah, I guess he is, but we have to keep him. He is one of our biggest clients."

"Oh I know, but he sure is stubborn! Why didn't Jeff warn me about him? I have shown him several ideas and he shoots down every one. I think it's just because I'm a woman."

Andy laughed at the truth to her statement, "And a fine looking woman you are?"

Susan blushed, "Yeah right, Andy"

"Come on Susan, you know you are the most beautiful woman I have ever laid eyes on."

Susan sighed, "Don't start with me, Andy. I must not have been too fine for you to have…oh never mind! Just forget it."

Andy let it drop; knowing that now was not the time to talk about it. He didn't want to get her worked up before the meeting. "Well anyway, Susan, the meeting is in the conference room at two o'clock today. Don't be late and please bring some ideas with you."

"That old geezer has shot down all of my ideas."

Andy asked, "Try to come up with a few more before the meeting, please."

"Okay," Susan said, "I'll pull one right out of my butt, how's that?" She knew she probably shouldn't have said that to her boss, but she was talking to Andy and he knew she always spoke her mind, especially when she was upset.

Andy laughed, "Oh Susan! I'll see you at 2 o'clock."

Susan sat at her desk fuming when Jan came in. "Oh my, you had the boss in here. What's going on?"

Susan told her all about the meeting and the jerk of a client. Jan said, "Oh bummer! I was hoping he liked you and y'all were going out."

Susan giggled, "Nope, sorry to disappoint you." She didn't tell Jan that they already had a past, she didn't think anyone at work should know, plus it really wasn't any of their business.

Jan asked, "Well, are you ready for lunch?"

"Sorry Jan, it looks like I will be working through lunch today, thanks to the boss. I have to have some new ideas ready to pitch in time for the meeting because that old goat has shot all my other ideas down."

Jan laughed and asked, "Susan is it a good idea to call the boss an old goat?"

Susan shook her head, "No, not him, the client, mean old Mr. Jones."

"Oh!" Jan said, "Yeah he has always been a handful even for Jeff."

"Yea, well Jeff forgot to tell me anything about him."

Jan giggled and said, "Maybe he was afraid you wouldn't take the job if he did. Do you want me to bring you a sandwich back?"

"No thanks, I wouldn't have time to eat it anyway. I have to come up with a few new ideas by two o'clock."

"Yuck," Jan said, "I'll talk to ya later."

Susan got to work, she had one hour left and couldn't come up with much worth pitching. At five till two, Susan packed up the ideas she had come up with and straightened her clothes and headed to the elevator. She was determined to get this client, she thought, you know what old man I'll have you eating out of my hand before we are done. She stood in front of the closed conference room door having an attack of the nerves. She could hear Mr. Jones and Andy in the room talking and he sounded like a normal person, so why was he so mean to her? Was he a male chauvinist or something? She took a deep breath and opened the door, as she walked in, Andy and Mr. Jones both stood. Andy introduced them and she reached out to shake Mr. Jones hand. After the introductions were done, Andy asked them both to have a seat.

Mr. Jones said, "You are awful young Miss."

"Susan please, you may call me Susan."

"Okay Susan, you are very young. Mr. Boyd, Are you sure she is qualified for this job?"

Andy replied, "Yes, Mr. Jones, I have known Susan for a very long time, she has her college degree and very respectable job history and she is very, very, good at her job." Susan was fuming; they were talking about her like she wasn't even there. She looked over at Andy and he could tell she was about ready to blow so he said, "Susan, please show us what you have come up with."

Susan started to argue but Andy said, "We can do this Susan." He leaned down and gave her a light kiss on the cheek and told her to stop worrying. Susan gathered her things and left. She didn't even go back to her office, she just headed home. Oh No! I'm in trouble, she thought as she touched her cheek. Andy had set her on fire once again. She thought she was over him but it didn't appear to be the case. This was not good not good at all. What in the heck was she going to do? She had to work with him all week, alone, just the two of them. This was not good.

Susan drove home and spent her afternoon relaxing and thinking about how she was going to deal with Andy for the rest of the week. Later that night she talked to Vickie about it, Vickie convinced her she could do it and not to worry about her and Andy. If it was meant for her and Andy to get back together, they would, and if not, then they wouldn't. It did not matter where she worked. The next day Susan had convinced herself she could do this, besides she and Andy had a long history, they had been friends forever.

Chapter Twenty-Seven

Susan wore one of her best dresses the next day; it made her look good, which made her feel more confident. She wouldn't admit that she was dressing up for him, but he was the one who messed up, so if she could torture him a bit, she would. Her legs were tan so she didn't wear pantyhose; in fact she hated panty hose. Her dress was a light blue, barely above her knees, and low cut in the front. She wore nice low heels in silver and long dangly silver earrings to accompany her dress. As she walked into her office the phone rang, it was Andy.

"Hi Susan, come on up to my office. The rest of this week we will be working up here. My office is bigger than yours and I want to get started right away."

'I'll be right up."

Just as she was leaving her office, Jan came by and asked, "Where ya going Chickie?"

Susan told her, "I'll be working in Mr. Boyd's office for the rest of the week," then she proceeded to tell her about the meeting yesterday and why she had to work with him this week.

Jan said, "Wow! You go girl, maybe he will fall for you while y'all are working together. I mean he's hot, I would love to work with him all week."

Susan smiled and said, "I'll see ya later."

The first two days of working together flew by, Andy sat behind his desk and she sat across from him with a laptop. Working with Andy was not bad at all their pitch was coming along better than she had expected. Little did she know, it was killing him to be that close to her and not be able to hold her and tell her how beautiful she was. She looked up and caught him staring at her.

"What?"

Andy said, "It's nothing, I was just thinking how nice this week has been having you in here working alongside me."

"Well don't get used to it, we only have two days left after today then I get to go back to my office. Do you think Mr. Jones will like what we have come up with?"

"Yes I do, he's just a little hard to deal with sometimes. Once you and him get used to each other it will be fine."

"Oh! I don't know about that. I don't think he likes me very much."

"Well then on Monday wear your prettiest, sexiest dress ever and he will be so blinded by lust and you will have him eating out of your hand."

Susan laughed right out loud at that and said, "Oh yeah, I bet."

Andy said, "It's a bet, do it and let's see what happens, if I win, you have to have supper with me that night to celebrate."

Susan said, "You're on, but if I win I get a raise"

Andy laughed and said, "You will have earned it anyway, but okay. It's time we head out, this day is over are you ready?"

"Sure" Susan said.

"I'll walk you out. Do you need a ride home?"

"No, but thanks for asking. I have my own car."

They rode the elevator in silence, then while walking her to the car Andy asked, "Susan, are you ever going to forgive me?"

Susan stopped and looked at him, "I already have, a long time ago. It's just hard for me to trust you again."

He leaned in to her and lightly kissed her and said, "I hope one day I can help you learn to trust me again, I miss you."

"I miss you too, Andy, goodbye," she walked away heading to her car. As she got in her car, she looked in the rearview mirror wondering if she should risk trusting him again. It was clear, she still had feelings for him, but could she let herself believe in him again. Obviously, he had moved on, she had seen all of the tabloids showing him with all the different women he had dated. He was rich now and she was far from it and there were so many more women that are prettier than her out there. She couldn't understand why he even cared about her anymore, unless it was just because he wanted her again to prove to her he could still have her, to crush her again. She was going to have to be careful because he would be right, if she let herself get involved with him again. It had hurt her too much the first time, could she risk getting hurt again. Touching her lips where he had kissed her brought back so many memories. Pulling out of the parking garage, Susan headed home. Two more days, that's all she had left to work that closely with him, then she could go back to her own office and going back to avoiding him again.

Andy watched her drive away and thought to himself, I'm going to make you fall in love with me again. He still loved her, it was hard for him to admit it, but he did. He was going to get to her, somehow, he had to. He had not been complete since they broke up, if that's what you wanted to call it, or since he had messed up. Oh he had tried to forget her and move on; he even thought he had until he had seen her asleep in the hospital. Even then he could fight his feelings, but when she started working here, he knew he was lost. He had fought it long enough, now it was time to fight for her. He planned on winning too, she was a fine woman, one any man would be proud to have and he wanted her. Tony had, had her for four years and he hadn't even bought her a ring, at least he'd never seen her wearing one, so it was time for him to show her that he was the one she was meant to be with.

The next two days flew by' they had everything planned for their meeting on Monday. It was Friday and like the last two days, they walked out together. In the parking garage Andy stopped her, turned her around, and kissed her lightly on the lips. He told her "I've been waiting to do that ever since I did it on Wednesday."

Susan asked him, "What stopped you?"

"You are still with Tony, I don't want to hurt or confuse you. I made Tony promise me that he would never hurt you, and what kind of person would I be if I hurt you again? I swore I would stay away from you, but this week has been hell, I miss you so much and I would do anything if you would give me another chance to prove to you just how much you still mean to me"

"Oh Andy, you idiot! I haven't been with Tony in over two years. He and I are just friends, we just were just not meant to be."

He smiled and pulled her roughly into his arms and really kissed her, like he was starving for her. In fact Susan could have sworn her toes had just curled up, dang he's good.

Andy asked, "What are your plans this weekend?"

Susan told him, "I am going to my parents tonight but don't have plans for the rest of the weekend."

Andy said, "Let's drive up to the craft fair tomorrow and have a little fun for a change. We've been cooped up all week together working on this project and we survived. I think we have earned the right to have a little fun, what do you say?"

Susan wanted to say no, she just wasn't ready, "I don't know."

He pleaded with her, "Come on Susan, it'll be fun. I promise nothing will happen that you don't want to happen."

Susan smiled and said, "Fine, you win! Pick me up at ten o'clock," then gave him her address.

He smiled and pulled her into his arms for one more kiss before he told her goodbye and watched her walk to her car. He loved watching her walk; she could bring any man to his knees with her walk. The way she sways her hips without even knowing she's doing it made him melt. Man she was hot, he had to go home and take a cold shower just to put out the fire.

Andy drove up to her apartment the next day and knocked on her door at ten o'clock on the dot. Susan had overslept, she got up, jumped in the shower, and wasn't even ready when he showed up. She threw on a robe and went to answer the door. She told him, "Come on in for a minute, I'm almost ready. Have a seat." She ran back to her room, put on a pair of short shorts that she knew would drive him crazy and a tight tank top with flip flops. She braided her hair and threw on some mascara and took off down the hall to meet him in the living room. He had heard her come in so he turned around and said, "Oh God! Susan you look good enough to eat."

Susan giggled and said, "Are you ready?"

Andy said, "Yeah, come on let's go" he took her by the arm and led her to his car, he opened the door and helped her in. Andy walked around and got in the car and Susan asked. "what happen to your truck?"

"I traded it in a long time ago, I wanted a sports car."

"I love it," she said and settled down into the soft leather seats that smelled so good.

They drove a while until they found the craft fair; it was on a road beside the beach that would attract the attention of all the sunbathers too. They parked and he came around to help her out. As they started walking, he took her hand. She didn't mind, it felt good to hold his hand and she was enjoying herself.

Andy said "This is nice."

Yes," Susan agreed as they walked by the booths looking at the crafts and talking. She was laughing and having a good time and Andy was too.

Susan said, "I'm hungry, let's find something close by to snack on."

They found a booth that had burgers and hotdogs so they grabbed a couple of hot dogs and sat on a bench to eat.

"These are so good, I always like them better when you buy them out like this rather than fixing them at home," Susan said.

"Yeah, I remember that, they are really good," Andy said.

After they finished their hot dogs, they walked around some more and came upon a booth that caught Susan's attention, she had always loved jewelry. As she wandered over to it Andy said, "Look at this Susan it looks like something you would wear."

She turned and saw a long silver chain with a beautiful lighthouse on it. She looked up at Andy with tears in her eyes and said, "It's beautiful," she didn't have to tell Andy that it made her immediately think of his home.

"That settles it then, I'm buying it for you."

"You don't have to do that" she said.

"I know but I want to," so he gave the lady the money then told Susan, "Turn around." She turned and lifted her hair out of the way and he placed it around her neck then bent to place a small kiss on her neck and told her it was where it should be and that it looked lovely on her. She turned back around and looked at him with unshed tears in her eyes, "Thank you."

Andy told her she was welcome then pulled her hand and said, "Come on, we still have more to look at," and so they started off down the street again. After about two more hours of walking they decided they had seen enough and headed back to the car.

"This has been fun" Susan said, "I'm glad I came."

"Me too" Andy said as he opened the car door for her. After she got in he went around and got in on his side and he asked her if she was up for going to supper while they were out and she said agreed.

Andy said, "I found this quite little place, I think you will like, and we won't have to dress up so we can go just as we are."

Chapter Twenty Eight

They pulled up at a nice little bar; he parked, came around and opened her door.

"WOW! This is a really cute place," Susan remarked.

"Yeah, I thought you might like it, I found it on my way to a business meeting one day."

They walked in and to Susan's surprise the place was pretty busy. They found a small table in the back and a waitress immediately came up to take their drink orders and handed them a menu. Susan ordered a coke and Andy a root beer. The waitress went off to get the drinks while they looked over the menu.

Susan asked, "Andy what are you getting?"

"Hmm, I think I will get a big cheeseburger and fries."

Susan laughed and said, "A man after my own heart."

Andy looked at her, suddenly serious, and said, "Yes I am Susan, I miss you."

The waitress decided to return at that time and Susan broke eye contact to give the waitress her order. While they were waiting on their food, Andy said, "Let's dance," he held out his hand and Susan placed hers in his. Andy got up led Susan to the dance floor just as one of their old favorite songs came on. She looked up at him and he just looked at her, pulling her into his arms and said, "This is like old times, I couldn't have picked a better song." Susan relaxed and put her head on his shoulder as she got into the music. Just being in his arms again felt so right after all these years, could it be that she could trust him again? It felt so good as she looked up and he looked down into her eyes.

Susan could see the desire he felt for her, and strangely enough, she could see tears forming in his eyes. Andy pulled her in closer and said, "I have missed you so much, I would give anything to not have messed up like I did. I have never stopped loving you, Susan."

Susan was so touched; he brought tears to her eyes as she leaned into him. He leaned down to kiss her and his kiss was one of the most thrilling kisses she had ever had in her life, she felt sparks all the way down to her toes, her knees went weak and he held her up until she got her balance back and then he said, "Our food is here are you hungry?"

She looked up into his eyes and said, "Yes," and she didn't just mean for food either. Susan wondered if Andy could see the desire in her eyes and if he knew that she was hungry for far more than the food before her. They walked back to the table and he helped her into her chair and then went around to his chair. As they ate their supper, they talked about all of the things they had seen that day.

After supper, Andy took Susan home, walking her up to the door. He kissed her goodnight reminded her, "Remember, wear a knock em out dress on Monday for our meeting with the old geezer as you call him."

Susan laughed and said, "I will see you then, thanks for a great day and night."

Sunday came and went. Susan slept in that day then went to her mom and dad's for supper. She thought about what she should wear to the meeting the next morning and what Andy had said about dressing to knock his socks off. Susan decided she had a better plan, laughing she wondered what Andy would think when she came in to the meeting wearing this outfit.. Wondering if this outfit would be more to Mr. Jones liking, she couldn't wait to find out the next morning and she headed to bed.

The next morning Susan got up, showered, had breakfast, and took great care putting her make up on and her very special perfume. Then she dressed and headed to work. As she got to her office, Jan whistled said, "Girl you look like you are on a mission."

Susan said, "I am, I have that meeting today with our boss and Mr. Jones and I'm going to find out if he likes me better as a man or woman."

Jan laughed and said, "Good luck, I wish I could be a fly on the wall in there when you walk in."

Susan giggled and said, "Yeah I thought it would be a good plan, but now I'm nervous."

Jan said, "Don't be you will do fine."

It was time for the meeting and Susan rode the elevator up, she had hid from Andy all morning because she didn't want him to see what she was wearing before the meeting. She had got a lot of weird looks from her associates but she hoped it would play out good in the meeting. As she approached the conference room, she heard their voices; she stopped, straightened her coat, and opened the door. Both men stopped talking and looked up at her, Andy almost started laughing but covered it with a cough as she glared at him.

"Hello gentlemen are we ready to start this morning?"

Mr. Jones looked at Andy, he just shrugged his shoulders and said, "Sure."

After the meeting Mr. Jones said "He loved their idea, but he had a couple of questions."

Andy said, "Okay, let's hear them."

He said, "Oh they are not for you, they are for Miss. Lewis."

Susan said, "Okay, what can I do for you?"

He grinned and said, "Should I call you Mr. or Miss. Lewis now?"

Andy laughed and Susan said, "You may call me Susan"

Mr. Jones said, "Okay but I got to tell you, that's not a good name for a man."

She said, "I only dressed this way to try making you feel more comfortable, you didn't seem to like me very much last time."

He laughed and said, "Well darling, I like you just fine now! Anyone who would go the extra mile for me has my approval. I gotta tell ya something though."

"What's that," she asked?

He laughed and said, "I never smelled a man that smelled so dang good and never in my life have I ever seen one that could wear them sexy high heels and walk around on them without falling. Why you women torture your feet is beyond me."

Andy roared with suppressed laughter and Mr. Jones joined in. Susan just laughed with them. She said, "Well at least I got your attention."

He said, "Honey, you had my attention the first time I ever met you, if I was a few years younger I'd have you…well never mind. I'd just give anyone a run for their money."

She and Andy both laughed and Mr. Jones stood pulling her into his arms. He gave her a hug and said, "In the future, I think we will get along just fine."

She said, "Really?"

He laughed and said, "Yes ma'am, just be yourself and keep coming up with them ideas and we will get along just fine."

She gave him a hug back and said, "You've got a deal."

After he left, Andy shut the door and pulled her into his arms, he said, "You did it Susan, you got the contract! I knew you could do it."

She smiled and said, "Thank you, I believe you owe me a raise"

He laughed and said, "I think so too. I can't believe you wore a man's suit and got away with it. Only you, but did you forget that men don't wear high heels, or perfume?"

Susan laughed and said, "I actually never even thought about it, I can't believe he loved that."

Andy roared, "Honey he more than loved it, I think it turned him on. Didn't you see the way he sniffed you when you leaned over him?"

"Why Andy I think you're jealous?"

"You're darned right I am," grabbing her and pulling her in his arms he lowered his head and said, "You're mine and now that I've got you back, I'm never letting you go again."

Susan giggled and said "who said you have me back and that I want to be yours?"

He leaned down and kissed her so deep that her legs gave out so she raised her arms around his neck to hold on. After he finally broke the kiss he said, "Well?"

"Ok you've got me now, what are you going to do with me?"

Andy grinned and said, "Let me show you." He locked the door and started towards her, throwing everything off the table and pulled her into his arms. He kissed her until she was so turned on that she couldn't do anything but whimper with desire. He laid her back on the table and started undressing her, revealing her very feminine body underneath her masculine attire. He threw her suit to the floor drinking is his fill in with his eyes. He had waited so long to see her gorgeous body in this way, "God, you are so beautiful."

Susan smiled and raised her arms up to pull him close as he leaned over to kiss her. He pulled her to the edge of the table and worshipped her body before he took her to heaven. As they lay there catching their breath, he said, "Susan I love you, I always have and I always will." He looked into her eyes and asked, "Will you marry me?"

Susan smiled saying, "I love you too! I thought you'd never ask, of course I will marry you Anderson Boyd!"

The End.

Epilogue

It's a beautiful spring day on the gulf coast of Florida. It's been almost a year since Andy proposed. Susan wanted to wait until spring to get married when the flowers would all be in full bloom. Andy agreed with her, he really wouldn't deny her anything she wanted, so a spring wedding was fine with him. Today was the big day, they were getting married at sunset on the beach. They were having a small ceremony surrounded by their friends and family.

Susan was so excited, Vickie was her maid of honor and Carol came home to be her bridesmaid. Carol gotten into town two days ago and Susan and Vickie were so excited to see her. She was staying with them at her and Vickie's place. They had spent the last two days shopping, talking, and getting caught up. Susan was secretly hoping that she and Vickie, along with Carol's parents could talk her into moving back home. So far they hadn't had much luck, Carol admitted to missing everyone but said she loved New York.

The girls had given her a surprise bachelorette party last night, it was just Susan, Vickie, and Carol. She loved it, they had a blast hanging out, catching up and just doing girl stuff. The girls couldn't believe how much Susan's life had come full circle. She was getting married!

It was almost time for the girls to get into their dresses. Her mom and dad had rented a house on the beach for them to get dressed in. Andy rented one for himself and the groom's party to get dressed in as well. She hadn't seen him in two days. He was so busy planning their honeymoon which was going to be a surprise for her. She had no idea where they were going, but as long as they were together she would love it.

Vickie and Carol slipped into their dresses before they had to help Susan get into her wedding gown. Susan had picked pastel colored gowns for Carol and Vickie to wear today. Carol wore a light lavender dress while Vickie's was a pale melon color. They both looked beautiful in them. She tried to pick the color that would be most flattering to each of them and still fit in with their wedding theme.

Susan's dress was a gorgeous white concoction that would take Andy's breath away. The second she had laid her eyes on the pearl encrusted gown, she knew it was the one, it was the dress she had dreamed about since she was sixteen years old and Andy told her not to worry about the cost. She nearly didn't buy it because of the cost, but Andy told her that money was no object,, if she loved the dress, she was to buy it, and she knew that he couldn't wait to see her in it.

Susan was still getting used to the idea that she would never have to worry about money again. Andy was truly a self-made man who had gone from being orphaned at 13 years old, to a millionaire by 25.

She didn't have any intention of living extravagantly, but knowing that she would be able to live comfortably in their lighthouse for the rest of her life was all she needed.

Peeking out the windows of the rental house, Susan could see that the chairs were set up on the beach looking out over the water. They had planned it just right and they were saying their vows just as the sun was setting. The sunset over the water was an amazing sight, all the colors look like they were melting into the water. It would be perfect.

Susan had loved Andy nearly all of her life and she had waited so long for this day. She was so happy she knew they would have an amazing life together and she had the best wedding gift for him tonight, she couldn't wait to tell him what it was. As Susan looked out over the beach where she would become Mrs. Anderson Boyd, she could see that some of her guests had started to arrive. When she saw Tony walk onto the beach, her heart was full, her best friends were all here to celebrate with her today and she would be marrying her best friend in just a few short moments.

Susan was drawn back from the window by a knock on the door; her girls rushed her out of the room so they could see who was at the door. Susan's dad came into the room where she was hiding and his eyes immediately filled with tears, "Oh Susan, my beautiful baby girl, look at you! You are all grown up and a vision in that gown. I can't believe you are getting married, where did the years go?" Susan flew into his arms and clung to him in a way she hadn't done since childhood.

"Oh Daddy, I will always be your baby girl! I love you so so much, but you have to stop crying or I am going to destroy my make-up."

Carol and Vickie knocked on the door and peeked in, "Are you ready to go Susan? It's time!" Susan wiped her eyes with her grandmother's hankie, tucked her arm through her dad's and said, "Let's do this, my groom is waiting!"